No Comparison

Melodie's mother is Constance King, the big Broadway star. She starred in three different Rodgers and Hammerstein musicals, and she's done five TV specials, as well as a couple of movies.

I used to like visiting Melodie when her parents were still married. Connie is so pretty and she always makes a big fuss about me, just because I'm Melodie's friend. And Melodie's father is a lot of fun. He's Trevor Ashford and he's from England, so he has this wonderful accent. Melodie can talk like that if she wants.

I guess I've always been just a little jealous of Melodie. For starters, there's her name. Melodie St. Clare Ashford. Melodie almost never uses the St. Clare, which is some sort of old family name, but I think it's just wonderful. I personally am named Elaine Marissa Zuckerman, and even with the Marissa in the middle, there's no comparison.

**Other Apple® Paperbacks
you will enjoy:**

Truth or Dare
  by Susan Beth Pfeffer

Friends Are Like That
  by Patricia Hermes

A Season of Secrets
  by Alison Cragin Herzig
  and Jane Lawrence Mali

Starstruck
  by Marissa Gioffre

The Trouble with Soap
  by Margery Cuyler

Adorable Sunday
  by Marlene Fanta Shyer

Starting *with Melodie*

Susan Beth Pfeffer

AN
APPLE®
PAPERBACK

SCHOLASTIC INC.
New York Toronto London Auckland Sydney

ISBN 0-590-32198-6

12 11 10 9 8 7 6 5 4 3 2 1   12   5 6 7 8 9/8 0/9

Printed in the U.S.A.   06

Chapter

1

Just like always, Tuesday night I had supper at Melodie's.

I don't know when I got into the habit, but I've been doing it for years now, maybe for as long as Melodie and I have been best friends, and that's since third grade. We've shared a lot of suppers together, Tuesdays at her house and Fridays at mine, in the past seven years.

"Ritual is important to Melodie," my mother said once to my father when he said it would be nice to see me for supper some Tuesday night. "Especially now."

We all knew what she meant by "now." Last year, Melodie's parents decided to get a divorce, and things have been shaky at her house ever since. Not just for Melodie, but also for Lissa, her little sister.

It's not that people don't get divorced where we live. Couples split up all the time. Parents, teachers, older brothers and sisters, aunts, uncles, doctors, even the owners of the little Mom-and-Pop candy store. But when they split up it usually isn't in the papers, the way it's been with Melodie's parents. And usually the divorce follows a normal course. Husband moves out, wife keeps the kids, gets a job, and sometimes moves out of town because she can't afford to live there anymore. I've lost a lot of friends that way.

There was no question that Melodie's mother could afford to continue living in Morganville. Even without Melodie's father's income, they wouldn't suffer financially. Melodie's mother is Constance King, the big Broadway star. She starred in three different Rodgers and Hammerstein musicals (one was a revival, and everybody said she was better than the woman who starred in it originally, thirty years ago), and she's done five TV specials, as well as a couple of movies. Right now she's starring in *Shooting Stars!* on Broadway. The reviews said it was just a vehicle for her, but it's been sold out ever since previews, and if Connie wants she can play in it forever.

I used to like visiting Melodie when her parents were still married. Connie is so pretty and she always makes a big fuss about me, just because I'm Melodie's friend. And Melodie's father is a lot of fun. He's Trevor Ashford and he's from England, so he has this wonderful accent. Melodie can talk like that if she wants.

Trevor is a producer who does lots of big movie work. He's always getting international casts together and putting them in war movies. Melodie says that if he'd stayed in England he'd have been knighted by now, but she doesn't think that if he were Sir Trevor Ashford she'd be Lady Melodie, so I can't see the point.

The thing about Melodie is that she could really carry being Lady Melodie Ashford. I guess I've always been just a little jealous of her. For starters, there's her name. Melodie St. Clare Ashford. It sounds like it fell out of a Gothic novel. Melodie almost never uses the St. Clare, which is some sort of old family name, but I think it's just wonderful. I personally am named Elaine Marissa Zuckerman, and even with the Marissa in the middle, there's no comparison.

"Maybe you could drop the Elaine," Melodie suggested once. She's always been very sympathetic about my name. "You could just be Marissa Zuckerman."

"That sounds good," I said. "Especially if you leave out the Zuckerman. Maybe I could just be Marissa. I could design jeans with a name like Marissa."

"Or sheets," Melodie said. "Like Mama."

That's what I mean about Melodie's family. One day a big fabric company called up Connie and asked her to design sheets for them. So now people can go into department stores and buy Constance King sheets. I don't like them all that much, because they have lots of little flowers all over them and I like geometric designs better, but even so. Can you imagine having sheets named after you in bedrooms all over this country? Who would buy Elaine Zuckerman sheets?

Melodie's little sister, Lissa, is really named Melissa Penelope Ashford, which I don't think is quite as good as Melodie St. Clare, but it's a pretty good second. Penelope is Trevor's extremely British mother. She comes to visit once a year for two weeks and makes Connie a nervous wreck, but Melodie and

3

Lissa and I like her. She insists on tea every afternoon, the way the British do it, and she tells us stories about Queen Elizabeth and Prince Philip as if she knew them. Connie swears up and down that Penelope never met the royal family, but it doesn't matter. Connie met them at a command performance once, but her stories about them aren't nearly as interesting.

My own grandparents live in Florida and California, and when they come up to visit, things get a little more crowded and a lot noisier. When we go to Florida or California to see them, it's even worse because they live in apartments and there isn't nearly enough room for all of us. We end up scrunched together, and soon we're all screaming at one another, and then we cry, and then we make up, and then we scream all over again. Each year my mother swears we aren't going to do it again, and each year we do. I can't be sure how it is when Melodie visits Penelope in England, but I can't picture Penelope ever screaming.

Another reason I'm jealous of Melodie is her house. I love where she lives. It's a mansion, with a genuine music room and tons of antiques. I love my own house, too, but Mom has her office on the side of the house, and when she gives her patients a shot of Novocain, sometimes you can hear them shriek. Even under the best of circumstances, having a dentist for a mother lacks glamour.

And Dad's business is no better. He's in computer chips. Lots of times he tries to explain *what* he is in computer chips, and I know I should pay more attention, but there's no way I'm ever going to go into computer chips for a living.

Trevor is always traveling around, going to London and Paris and Hollywood to make deals and get all those international stars together. Dad travels almost every week to Pittsburgh. His company had its corporate headquarters in Pittsburgh. What can you say about a business that makes Pittsburgh its corporate headquarters?

I rang the doorbell to Melodie's house that Tuesday night, and Miss Hardwick answered the door. She's Lissa's governess. She was Melodie's and when Melodie outgrew her Lissa was born, so she stayed on. "Hi, Elaine," Miss Hardwick said, smiling. "Come on in. Melodie is in her room."

"Thanks," I said. Even though I didn't know Miss Hardwick when she was Melodie's governess, she's one of those people I always associate with Melodie's life. A governess. She takes the girls to their doctors' appointments and has supper with them and helps them with their homework. Connie spends Tuesdays in New York City so she can be fresh for her Wednesday matinee, and she spends weekends there, as well. Having Miss Hardwick means she doesn't have to worry about the girls being home alone.

Alone means with Hans and Marta, the live-in couple. Hans is the chauffeur and gardener, and Marta does the cleaning and cooking. They scare me, but I love the idea of having live-in servants. We have a once-a-week cleaning lady who makes the house stink of cigarettes, even though she isn't supposed to smoke on the job. I always spray the house with Lysol after she leaves.

Since Melodie was upstairs, I went right up to her bedroom. Sure enough, she was lying on her bed, looking miserable. Melodie has spent a lot of time looking that way since her parents split up.

"What's happening?" I asked, sitting down on the bentwood rocker. Melodie's bedroom is very pretty, with lace curtains and pale blue walls, but I prefer my bedroom, which has lots of books and my mother's old desk—and geometric sheets.

"It's awful," Melodie said, barely looking at me. "Elaine, it's so awful. I just don't know what I'm going to do."

"What is it now?" I asked with a sigh. Being a best friend means putting up with a lot of complaining.

"It's Daddy, of course," Melodie said. "And Mama, for that matter."

All of Melodie's problems lately were Daddy and Mama. I missed the good old days when Melodie got hysterical because she made only an 89 on a test or because Karen Steiner said something mean about her in gym. Karen Steiner still says mean stuff, but Melodie doesn't seem to hear her. And her grades have fallen even below 89, but she doesn't care anymore.

"What is it now?" I asked, because Melodie expected me to. To be perfectly honest, Melodie has asked me her share of expected questions over the years. It isn't as if she never listens to my complaints.

"Daddy was supposed to be in town this weekend," Melodie said. "At his new apartment in New York City. And he asked Mama if Lissa and I could stay with him for the whole weekend. Maybe even take Friday off from school, so we'd have plenty of time for a visit. He's just back from Rome, and we haven't seen him in a couple of weeks."

6

"So what's the problem?" I asked.

"Well, things got complicated in Rome," Melodie said. "And Daddy called last week and said he didn't think he'd be back in New York this week, after all, and told Mama he couldn't see us, and we should make plans to see him next weekend instead. Only Mama got annoyed about that, because we were supposed to go to Boston and see her parents next weekend. Mama was supposed to fly there after her Sunday matinee and join us, and we were going to take Monday off from school and have a long weekend together."

Melodie never missed this much school when things were normal. No wonder her grades were slipping.

"Did your father get mad?" I asked.

"Sure," Melodie said. "But that isn't the problem."

"No?" I asked. Trevor has a fierce temper. I saw him lift a genuine Chippendale chair once, in a fit of anger, and throw it clear across the room. It cost a fortune to get it repaired. That day he was angry at the entire Yugoslavian army for taking too long filming a war movie.

"The problem is that Daddy called this morning from Rome," Melodie said, "and told Mama he was leaving Rome this afternoon and would be home tomorrow. He said he wanted Lissa and me to spend the weekend with him the way we'd originally planned. So Mama started shouting at him that he was unreliable and she couldn't trust him with us, and she wasn't going to let us anywhere near him this weekend, and if he tried to see us in Morganville she was going to get guard dogs and train them to kill him on sight."

7

Connie didn't need guard dogs as long as she had Hans and Marta. "I bet that really made Trevor angry," I said.

"We were in the breakfast room," Melodie said. "And Mama was on the phone in the den and I swear I could hear him shouting. I could certainly hear her. It was awful."

"Did Lissa hear?" I asked.

Melodie frowned. "She heard everything. She ran upstairs, crying, and it took Miss Hardwick hours to get her calmed down. Lissa didn't go to school today, she was so upset. And that made Mama even angrier, like it was all Daddy's fault, and she called her lawyer and said she wanted to get the custody situation settled immediately, so that Lissa and I would see Daddy only one weekend a month and for two weeks in the summer. And no trips with him to Europe, like we'd been promised."

"That's awful," I said. I knew how much Melodie's weekends with Trevor meant to her, and she'd really been looking forward to spending July with him in London. "Can she do that?"

"If she proves Daddy's really irresponsible," Melodie said. "At least that's what her lawyers say."

"But Trevor isn't irresponsible," I said. "Just busy."

"I know," Melodie said. "But Mama will call in all sorts of people who'll say Daddy is a terrible influence on us, because of all his women and everything. I like Daddy's girl friends, just as long as he doesn't think about marrying them."

Even my parents, who never gossip about Trevor

8

and Connie when they think I can overhear them, admit Trevor is a terrible womanizer. I'm not sure that's the only reason he and Connie split up, but it's been a convenient excuse for everything Connie's been doing ever since.

"Your father won't let Connie get away with that," I said, trying to soothe Melodie. I never felt comfortable when she started talking about her parents' problems. I'd already had a couple of years' practice and it still didn't feel right. "He can afford good lawyers, too, and they'll prove he's perfectly responsible and should be able to see you every weekend and all summer, just the way it was supposed to be."

"I'm really scared," Melodie said, sitting up on her bed. The bed had a big lace canopy, and she looked like she was sitting under a giant frilly tent. "Daddy's getting angry about the whole situation, and you know what he's like when he's angry."

If Trevor ever got really angry, even the guard dogs would be in trouble. I nodded.

"He and Mama have been fighting about when he can see us ever since he moved out," Melodie said. "And I know how much he wanted to see us this weekend. There's a benefit preview of his new movie on Saturday. It's for the Heart Fund, and Lissa and I were supposed to go with him. He's planned it for ages. And then Mama just arbitrarily decided we can't go because Daddy didn't give her enough warning that he was going to be home, after all."

"Maybe she'll change her mind," I said.

"Maybe," Melodie said. "But even if she does, Daddy'll stay mad. He doesn't like it when Mama changes her mind any more than she likes it when he does."

"They'll work it out," I said. "Maybe it'll take the lawyers to do it, but they both love you and Lissa, and that's the important thing. Everything will be okay. And I bet you get to go to London this summer just like you planned. Connie won't keep you from seeing your grandmother."

"I don't know," Melodie said. "She hates Penelope."

"My mother doesn't like Dad's mother, either," I said. "I think it has to do with being in-laws."

"At least your parents love each other," Melodie said. "And even if they didn't, they'd never act like this."

Last week I walked into the kitchen and found Mom and Dad kissing right in front of the refrigerator. So I guess they're not about to get divorced.

But even if they did, the stakes wouldn't be as high. I have to admit I wouldn't be devastated if Mom refused to let me spend July in Pittsburgh with Dad.

So even though I knew Melodie was miserable, I still couldn't help being a little bit jealous.

Chapter

2

One thing I have that Melodie doesn't is a boyfriend. His name is Steve Miller, and he's also a sophomore.

We met last year, when his family moved to Morganville from Portland. His father is a veterinarian, and his mother is a housewife. As far as I can tell, all she does is stay home and bake. She bakes all the time—cookies, cakes, brownies. My mother says she's God's gift to dentists.

Steve and I have been dating for a couple of months now, nothing too serious because my parents won't allow it, so only weekend dates—parties, movies, football games. I really like having a boyfriend and I especially like Steve. He's about five feet ten, with curly brown hair and hazel eyes. He does well in school and he wants to do something meaningful with his life. I don't know what I want to be yet, except that it won't have anything to do with teeth or computer chips.

"How about a movie Friday night?" Steve asked me, the day after I'd been to Melodie's. He and I were walking home from school, a parentally approved activity.

"I can't on Friday," I said. "You know that."

"What do I know?" Steve asked.

I couldn't tell whether he was being deliberately dumb or whether he really had forgotten. "Friday nights Melodie and Lissa always have supper with my family," I said. "And they spend the night at our house. Sometimes Melodie spends the whole weekend with me. Her mother is in the city, so there's no reason for Melodie to stay home."

"Sometimes I think you live with Melodie," Steve grumbled. "Besides, if she's over every Friday, she wouldn't mind skipping one. So how about it?"

"Why not Saturday night?" I asked.

"Because I can't Saturday night," he said. "My cousin Jenny is getting married and my whole family is going out of town to the wedding. We won't be back till late Sunday. It's Friday night or nothing."

"Then it's nothing," I said.

"Oh, come on, Elaine," he said. "One Friday night won't kill Melodie."

"You don't understand," I said. "This Friday night it's really important for Melodie to have a place to go to. She and Lissa were supposed to spend Friday night with their father, only there was a mix-up and her mother got angry, and now she won't let the girls spend the weekend with him. Melodie's really upset about it. If I tell her she can't stay at my place Friday night it'll be like everybody's betraying her."

"I think you're exaggerating," Steve said. "So she spends the night alone. She has her sister, and all those servants."

"There's only Marta and Hans," I said. "And Miss Hardwick."

Steve snorted. "That's more servants than most people have relatives," he said. "Melodie won't die from loneliness."

"No, Steve," I said. "Melodie is my best friend, and she's going through a bad time. I'm not going to desert her in her hour of need."

"But you'll desert me," he said. "Leave me all alone on a Friday night."

"You're deserting me for the rest of the weekend," I said. "For cousin Jenny's wedding. I didn't even know you had a cousin Jenny."

"I didn't either until we moved east," Steve said. "I swear I have more long-lost relatives than . . . than Melodie has servants."

We both laughed. "They're not Melodie's servants," I said. "They're Connie's. There's a difference."

"I don't see it," Steve said. "Besides, Melodie always acts like they're her servants. She's really stuck-up."

"No, she isn't," I said. "Melodie is the least stuck-up person I know."

"Your mother is the least stuck-up person I know," Steve said. "Your mother could strike up a conversation with a drunken bum. Especially if he's seen a UFO."

This is something embarrassing about my mother. She is a UFO nut. And she isn't subtle about it. She drives a Datsun with a license plate that says UFO 86, which means there are at least eighty-five equally crazy drivers out there. And when our movie theater showed *Close Encounters of the Third Kind*, she saw it eight times. They still know her there.

Mom reads everything she can find about UFOs, and she belongs to a UFO society that meets every Tuesday night. Mom has never seen a UFO, but it isn't for lack of trying. I hope when she finally does, I'll be fully grown and living in a different state.

Steve was right, though. Mom would talk to anybody about UFOs. She nudges herself into conversations about them with all sorts of strangers. She took a train home from the city once and got so involved in a UFO conversation with a nun that they both missed their stops. I try very hard not to take train rides with her, and I absolutely refuse to go with her to that movie theater. It's just too awful.

I wasn't sure what I should say to Steve, though. He probably thought it was great that Mom would talk to anybody about UFOs. She wasn't his mother, after all. His mother was home that very minute baking something wholesome and American, the way a mother should be.

But I also knew I didn't want to get Steve on the subject of Melodie. It drove me crazy that he didn't like her. I wasn't sure how Melodie felt about him, because for the past couple of months the only thing she talked about was her crazy parents. Even if she didn't like Steve, she probably wouldn't tell me, though. Melodie is very well bred. It comes with the name.

"This is awful," I said. "A whole weekend and we won't be able to see each other. How will I survive?"

"Maybe they could freeze you for the weekend," Steve said. "Then you could be reheated on Monday in time for school."

So I gave him a friendly punch on the right arm. Steve pulled my hand and twirled me around so we were facing each other. Then we kissed just long enough to get me thinking about how I could manage to see him during the weekend.

"I have it," I said, kind of breathlessly.

"What?" Steve said. We were only a few doors away from my house, and I was sure all the neighbors had watched us kissing. Probably Mom's patients had seen us, too, but I didn't care.

"Come on over Friday night for supper," I said. "Mom says there's always room for one more."

"You mean have supper with your family and Melodie and her sister?" Steve asked.

"Lissa," I said. "She's only seven, but she's so cute, you'll love her. Say yes, Steve. It'll be so much fun, and you'll get a chance to see how nice Melodie is. And my parents will get a chance to know you better, and we can see each other then."

"I don't know," he said. "Dinner with the family sounds kind of serious. I don't have to ask for your hand in marriage to get dessert, do I?"

"You don't want dessert at my house," I said. "Mom is on a cheddar cheese kick. She read that cheddar cheese keeps people from having cavities, and nowadays that's all we get to eat. Dessert is bound to be apples and cheddar cheese."

"Yummy," Steve said.

"But dinner will be okay," I said. "We do the whole Sabbath thing, so there's wine and candles and challah. You won't mind that, will you?"

"No," Steve said. "We'll be getting the same stuff Saturday night at Jenny's wedding. It'll be good practice."

"So you'll come?" I asked.

15

"Sure," Steve said. "If it's okay with your parents. You should check it out with them first."

"I will," I said. "But I know it'll be okay."

We walked the remaining few feet to my house and I asked him in. Steve thought about it for a moment, but then he decided he'd better get home and start his biology project. I thought about what his mother was probably baking at that very moment and wished I were going home with him. There's only so much cheddar cheese you can eat before you go crazy for cookies and cake.

But somehow my mother can always tell when I've had fudge or chocolate cream pie. I think it's the contented smile on my face. So I kissed Steve good-bye, nodded when he said he'd call me later that evening, and went into the house. As I unlocked the front door, I could hear the sounds of Mom's drill making its way through some poor sucker's tooth. What a welcome.

Not that things were any cheerier once I got inside. I hung my jacket in the coat closet, dumped my books on the living room sofa, and discovered that Mitch and Barry were in the room, both reading and totally oblivious to the fact that I was alive and in their presence.

I guess when I made out the list of things I had that Melodie didn't, I left out older brothers. I was too involved with the good stuff, like Steve, geometric sheets, and happily married parents. But I also have older brothers, two of them, which is two more than I care to have. I'd swap them for one sweet baby sister so fast it would make your head spin.

It isn't that Mitch and Barry are mean. I might like them more if they were. At least then they'd be aware I exist. I've been around for fifteen years now, and I don't think they've bothered to notice.

I can't help but notice them. First off, they're identical twins. I am the kid sister of the Zuckerman twins. That's how three-quarters of the kids at my high school know me.

And everybody at school knows them. They're famous for lots of reasons. All twins are famous at my school (there are two other pairs, but one isn't identical and people aren't quite as aware of them), but Barry and Mitch are even more so because, much as I hate to admit it, they're both good-looking. Girls are always throwing themselves at them, not much caring which one they catch (or get caught by). Mitch and Barry are both tall, with wavy, almost black hair, super dark brown eyes, and eyelashes that are about six inches longer than mine. Neither one has ever had a pimple in his whole life. And they have teeth a dentist mother can take pride in—big and white and sparkling.

They're also smart. I'm smart, too, and my grades have always been as good as theirs, but they're so flashy that teachers notice them. It would be hard not to, even though they don't dress alike and lots of times they're in different classes. Mom and Dad are very big on making sure they have separate identities.

It's a losing battle, though, because Mitch and Barry always like the exact same things. They both took trumpet lessons for years, and I can't even begin to describe how horrible that was. Just think of two trumpets being practiced on for seven straight years. Sometimes they'd practice at the same time, playing different pieces; and sometimes they'd practice separately, one right after the other, so the noise wasn't as awful but lasted twice as long. And then there was the chess kick. They started playing chess at the same time, and they played against each other every night after trumpet practice. At least they were quiet, but it was so quiet it was eerie. For two years the only words I ever heard them say were "Check!" and "Checkmate!"

Bad as the trumpets and the chess were, they were at least private. What's really put them on the map is their baseball-playing abilities. Mitch and Barry play for the high school team, and they're both so good that all sorts of colleges have offered them scholarships, separately and together. It's terrible. Mitch plays shortstop and Barry plays second base, so they're a double-play combination. They also bat three and four in the lineup. It's always Zuckerman to Zuckerman, or Zuckerman batting Zuckerman home. The local newspaper just loves them.

Mitch and Barry live in a world all their own, one into which I'm definitely not invited. I know they know they're part of this family, since Mitch has decided he wants to go into computer chips and Barry has wanted to be a dentist practically since birth. So they must know about Mom and Dad. But I'm not all that sure they know my name, and I'd swear they don't know what my middle name is.

"What's my middle name?" I asked Mitch right then, just to confirm my suspicions.

"What?" he asked, looking up. He seemed genuinely surprised that there was another person in the room.

"What's my middle name?" I asked.

"What's the matter?" he asked. "Don't you know it?"

"Of course I know it," I said. "Barry, what's my middle name?"

He seemed as surprised to find me in the room as Mitch had been. "Did you say something?" he asked.

"I asked you what my middle name is," I said. "Doesn't either of you know what it is?"

Mitch scratched his head thoughtfully. It was my sincerest wish that he and Barry both be bald by age nineteen. "Something with an M, I think," he said. "Mabel, maybe?"

"It is not Mabel!" I cried. "I don't believe either of you knows your very own sister's middle name."

"I was only two when you were born," Mitch said. "I wasn't into names. How old were you when she was born?" he asked Barry.

"Two," Barry said. "Besides, why should I know her middle name when I'm not that sure what her first name is?"

"Oh, I know that," Mitch said. "She was named for great-aunt Esther, so her name must be Esther."

"Esther Mabel," Barry said. "Esther Mabel Zuckerman. It has a nice ring to it."

I take it back. Sometimes Mitch and Barry *are* mean to me. I would have started a fight, but they always beat me when I do. In addition to everything else, they've always outnumbered me.

So instead, I asked, "When's Mom's last appointment? I have something important to ask her."

"She's working late tonight," Mitch said. "She said we should make our own supper."

"Dad's in Pittsburgh," Barry added.

"Dad's always in Pittsburgh," I said. "I swear, I feel like an orphan."

But they'd already stopped listening. I picked up my books from the sofa and started going upstairs, when the phone rang. It was the family number, so I picked it up.

"Hello, Elaine?" Melodie asked. She sounded awful.

"It's me," I said. "What's the matter?"

"Things are terrible," she whispered. "Daddy's back and he tried to come here to see us, and Hans wouldn't let him in and there was an awful scene. And when I tried to go outside to see him Marta wouldn't let me, and Miss Hardwick wasn't here because she and Lissa were at the library. At least Lissa didn't have to go through all this, but I feel like I'm a prisoner in my own house. Daddy was hysterical and threatening to call the police and Hans was shouting at him, and after Daddy left Marta called Mama at the theater and told her everything, and Mama really is going to buy guard dogs."

"Oh, no," I said. "Can I do anything?"

"I don't think so," she said. "I just had to talk to somebody. Things are so bad here, Elaine, and I know they're going to get worse. And there's nothing I can do to stop it."

Chapter
3

I really liked the idea of having Steve over for dinner. Neither Mom nor Dad is that great a cook, but for Friday night supper they make a special effort. The house is clean because the cleaning lady comes on Thursdays, and I've had enough time to Lysol out the cigarette smells. We use our good china, and there are candles on the table, and wine glasses, and everything looks formal and pretty.

And something about its being the Sabbath puts us all on our best behavior. So I figured Steve would never see us or our house looking better, and it felt like my first dinner party.

Miss Hardwick dropped Melodie and Lissa off and Mom invited her to stay for dinner, but she said no. Mom always invites Miss Hardwick, and Miss Hardwick always says no. It's all part of the ritual. Friday nights Miss Hardwick has off, and probably the last thing she wants to do is have dinner with us all; but Mom feels she has to ask, so she does, knowing she'll be turned down.

Melodie seemed a little depressed, but Lissa was all giggles, and she ran to Mitch and Barry and demanded they play with her. The weird thing is, they promptly did. I swear they never played with me, except when they were trying out new forms of torture, but they really love Lissa. So the three of them were roughhousing when Steve came.

I would have preferred that things be a little quieter when he came, but it was good to hear Lissa laughing. The way Melodie had been telling it, Lissa cried all the time. She looked perfectly okay to me, having a pillow fight with the twins. Melodie was sitting on the sofa, ignoring what was going on, and Mom and Dad were in the kitchen. So it was left to me to play hostess.

"Come on in," I said, suddenly feeling shy. Steve had been over to my house often enough, but this was his first real meal with my family. And Sabbath dinner was special. Steve seemed to know that; he was wearing a tie and a sports jacket. Barry and Mitch weren't that well dressed, but Steve didn't seem uncomfortable.

"Steve, you know Melodie," I said. I felt like a total idiot the minute the words left my mouth. Of course they knew each other. They had three classes together.

So he looked at me a little funny when he said, "Yeah, I know Melodie. Hi, Melodie."

"Hi, Steve," she said listlessly. I wanted to kick her. The whole point of the evening was to prove she wasn't stuck-up. She was going to have to liven up a lot more before Steve changed his mind.

"Mitch and Barry are playing with Lissa," I said, even though that was obvious. "You know Mitch and Barry."

"I can't tell which is which, though," Steve said.

"Mitch is in blue," I said. "And Barry has the brown shirt on." It's always easier to identify them by clothes than by the subtle ways in which they really do look different.

"Hi, Steve," Barry said, looking up from Lissa's pillow attack. "Good to see you."

"Hi," Steve said, and I could see he felt ill at ease. So I decided to play hostess some more.

"Sit down," I said. "Would you like something to eat or drink? Supper should be ready soon, but if you're hungry, there's plenty of cheddar cheese."

"No, thanks," Steve said, sitting down on the sofa next to Melodie. The two of them were so stiff they looked like mannequins.

"Time out," Barry said, and sat down on a chair opposite them. Lissa kept on slugging Mitch, who was laughing too hard to defend himself. "How are things going, Steve?"

"Okay," Steve said. "How does the ball club look this year?"

"Really strong," Barry said, relaxing in the chair. "With a combination like Mitch and me we're bound to win the championship."

"Oh, sure," Melodie said sarcastically. I wish she hadn't. She takes that tone with the twins, the same as I do, because they're practically her older brothers, too, but Steve might not realize that and think that she was just being snotty. I wished Melodie would change her entire personality immediately and become bouncy and lovable on the spot.

"What do you know?" Barry asked her. "You still think first base is some kind of makeup."

Melodie half smiled, and I sighed. That half-smile was probably the best she would do all night.

Mom came out of the kitchen then. "Hi, Steve," she said. "I'm glad you could come. Is there anything I can get you? I have some lovely cheddar cheese."

"No, thanks," Steve said. "Elaine's already offered me some."

"Dinner will be ready in a couple of minutes," she said, perching on the arm of Barry's chair. "I hope you like fish curry."

"That sounds great," Steve said.

"Good," Mom said, and there we all were with nothing to say. I hated it. Lissa and Mitch were still laughing, but that only made the rest of us seem stiffer.

"My husband made the curry," Mom said. "He makes a very good curry."

"Great," Steve said.

Melodie decided to break the silence. "What happened at your UFO meeting?" she asked Mom.

Mom's face immediately lit up. "It was fascinating," she said. "We had a special guest from New York who actually saw a UFO flying over the Empire State Building last year."

"Really?" Steve asked. "That sounds great."

"It was," Mom said. "He tried taking pictures of it, but the battery in his camera had run down, so nothing he got was really in focus. But if you looked at the pictures very carefully with a magnifying glass, you could see the UFO."

"What did it look like?" Steve asked. He sounded genuinely interested. But then again, he didn't have to listen to this garbage all the time.

"Sort of like a Frisbee," Mom said. "Of course, a lot of UFOs turn out to be Frisbees, which is always so embarrassing. But who could throw a Frisbee all the way over the Empire State Building?"

"King Kong?" Barry suggested.

Mom ignored him. She's as used to ignoring us as we are to ignoring her. "Only it obviously wasn't a Frisbee, because it had lights on it. Little blinking lights."

"How could you tell they were blinking?" I asked.

"If you squinted, you could see they were," Mom said. "The pictures really weren't very good, but I think that made the man's story all the more believable. Usually fakes are very carefully done, so they look real. It's the real stuff that's out of focus."

"Is that so?" Steve asked.

"Absolutely," Mom said. "One of the most fascinating UFO displays I ever saw was almost completely invisible. The photographer had forgotten her light meter and she had to guess at the aperture and she guessed wrong, so the pictures were all over-developed."

"Wow," Steve said.

I didn't trust his wow. "Don't you think supper is ready?" I asked. I guess Dad must have heard me, because he came out of the kitchen, wiping his hands on a dish towel, and told us to go into the dining room.

We all piled in there. Lissa held Mitch's hand and insisted on sitting next to him. Mitch pulled out her chair very politely and then shoved it back fast to the table, which only made Lissa giggle harder. Melodie half smiled again, and Steve at least chuckled. I couldn't cheer everybody up.

Dad, Mitch, Barry, and Steve all put on yarmulkes, and we stood at the table as Mom said the blessing for the candles. Dad poured the wine, and we all sang the blessing for that, and then drank from our wine glasses. We always have sweet wine, which not everybody likes, but Steve didn't seem to mind. Then Dad sliced the challah, we said the blessing for that, and the meal began in earnest.

Even though Melodie and Lissa aren't Jewish, they've had so many Sabbath dinners with us that they know all the prayers by heart. Steve knows them, too, so we all sounded good singing them. Sometimes when people are over who don't know the prayers, I get self-conscious singing them and I start to squeak.

Dad dished out the fish curry, and Mom passed the salad bowl around. We all took generous portions, then added the chutney and almonds. Steve looked a little unsure of himself, but he followed our example, and soon he, too, was mushing the curry and chutney together.

"You've been quiet tonight, Melodie," Dad said. "Anything interesting going on in your life?"

"Nothing worth talking about," she said. "Please pass the salt."

"Plenty interesting has happened to us," Mitch said. "Anyone care to hear?"

"Of course," Mom said, handing Melodie the salt. "What's going on?"

"For one thing, there was a scout from the Cleveland Indians at the game yesterday," Mitch said.

"Really?" Dad said. "Who were they scouting?"

"Us, rumor has it," Barry said.

"How did you do?" Steve asked.

"Mitch went three for four," Barry said. "I only went two for four, but I hit a three-run homer. And we made four double-plays, and Mitch made a fantastic catch of a line drive. Best play he's made all season."

"So why haven't the Cleveland Indians beaten down our door?" Dad asked. "It sounds like you're irresistible."

"It was just a rumor," Mitch said. "Maybe there really wasn't a scout there."

"Or maybe they're checking to see if their budget can accommodate both of us," Barry said. "Twins cost more."

"Tell me about it," Mom said. "We've been trying to afford them for years."

"Do you really think you'll sign with a major league team?" Steve asked. His eyes got really big at the thought.

"Not until they've both graduated from college, thank you," Dad said.

"And done postgraduate work," Mom said.

"But then they'll be too old to be ballplayers," Steve said. His eyes weren't sparkling anymore, and I had a feeling I'd suffered a real loss of status.

"So we'll go into managing, instead," Mitch said. "Barry can be the team dentist, too. That could be a real money-saver."

We all laughed, even Melodie. She looked as relaxed as I'd seen her in a long time. Lissa had giggled straight through supper and was still doing it.

I felt better about things after that, and we all got involved in the next conversation, which was about a

TV movie we'd all seen the night before. Lissa only listened, but Melodie and Barry really went at it, since she loved the movie and he thought it was dumb.

I was glad Melodie had something positive to say, even if it was just about a TV show. Her face lit up, and she looked so pretty explaining how well directed the show was. She didn't sound like a know-it-all, either, just like somebody who really did know. I was glad Steve had an opportunity to see Melodie looking that way.

"So what if it was competently made?" Barry was saying, when the doorbell rang. We all stared at one another.

"I didn't invite anybody," Mom said. "Did anyone here?"

We all shook our heads. "I'll get it," Mitch said, getting up from his chair. Lissa got up, too, and followed him to the front door.

We couldn't hear what Mitch said, but we certainly could hear Lissa. "Daddy!" she squealed. "Melodie, it's Daddy!"

Melodie ran to the hallway, and we all followed her. Steve was the last one there, but I guess when he realized everyone was going, he figured he might as well, too.

"Daddy," Melodie said, and then ran to him and hugged him. "Daddy, it's so good to see you."

"Hi, loves," Trevor said, embracing Melodie and Lissa both. "Oh, lordy, it's good to see you."

"Come on in," Dad said, and soon we were back in the living room. We didn't sit down, though.

"I hope I haven't interrupted your dinner," Trevor said. "I know it's terribly rude of me to drop in like this, but I'm just back from Rome, and I want to see my daughters. I knew they'd be here, so I came right over."

"How have you been, Trevor?" Mom asked. I realized then that she was feeling uncomfortable with the situation. I wasn't used to that. Mom can handle anything.

"Just fine, Doris," he replied. "Rome was a zoo, but Rome is always a zoo. Nothing new there."

"Are you home for a while now?" Dad asked. He looked like he might suggest we all sit down, but he didn't. I guess he was taking his cues from Mom, and she was looking less and less happy.

"For at least a month," Trevor said. "Probably more. The new movie seems to be under control, and I don't really think they'll need me there for a while. I might have to fly off for a couple of days next week, but that hardly counts."

"Hardly," Mom said.

"Does Mama know you're here?" Melodie asked, breaking away from her father.

"She wasn't the first person I thought of telling," Trevor said. "Frankly, I don't think she much cares."

"She'll want to know that we've seen you," Melodie said.

"Ah, darling, don't be such a spoilsport," Trevor said, and he gave Melodie a dazzling smile. Connie wasn't the only one in that family who could dazzle. "I wanted to see my daughters. As a matter of fact, we have a date for tomorrow night. I thought if the

29

Zuckermans didn't mind I'd take my two beauties home with me tonight, just as we'd originally planned, and then tomorrow we could shop for dresses for the benefit."

"What are you talking about?" Mom asked.

"The girls were scheduled to spend the weekend with me," Trevor said. "And then there was a little mix-up, and I wasn't sure I'd be back in time. But I am, and the girls are available, and we're all supposed to go to a benefit preview of my new film tomorrow night. If you and Don would like to come, I'm sure I can squeeze a couple of tickets out of some society lady."

"Does Connie know about this?" Mom asked.

"Certainly she knows," Trevor said. "Really, Doris, I'm not going to steal my daughters. I do have visitation rights, and I'm supposed to have the girls this weekend."

"It's all right, Doris," Melodie said. "Mama knows all about it. Lissa and I are supposed to spend the weekend with Daddy. It was arranged ages ago."

Mom pursed her lips. "I don't suppose there's any way we can get in touch with Connie to check it out," she said.

"Mama's just started her show," Melodie said. "Really, Doris, it's all arranged. Mama probably didn't think to tell you because she didn't know Daddy would be home in time." She gave Mom a wistful look.

"I want to go to the benefit," Lissa said. "Daddy promised we could go. I'll get to stay up till after midnight."

"She'll fall asleep by ten," Trevor said, giving Lissa a hug. "And I'll end up carrying her for the entire evening. But I want to show off both my beauties."

"Trevor, we can't let you take the girls without clearing it with Connie first," Mom said. "You must realize that."

"I realize no such thing," he said. "I'm their father, after all. I have rights, too."

"Doris, please let us go with Daddy," Melodie said.

"Honey, I can't," Mom said. "If you're willing to wait here until after Connie's performance, I'll call her up then and see if it's all right with her."

"I have no intention of waiting here for three hours just to get Her Highness's permission," Trevor said. "Melodie, Lissa, get your coats. We're leaving here immediately."

"Come on, Trevor," Dad said, putting his hand on Trevor's arm. "It's just a couple of hours. There's plenty of food here, and it'll give us a chance to catch up on your news."

"Girls, get your coats," Trevor repeated, brushing Dad's hand off. "Don, Doris, I appreciate your concern, but my daughters and I have plans for this weekend, and we intend to see them through."

"If you leave with the girls, I'll have to call Connie at the theater," Dad said. "And she might make a big stink about it."

"That's her problem," Trevor said.

"Don't do this, Trevor," Mom said. "You're only making a bad situation worse."

"Thanks for your advice," he said. "Girls, we are

31

leaving in ten seconds. Either put on your coats or prepare to be chilly."

Lissa and Melodie looked at my parents for a moment, then at their father. First Melodie, and then Lissa, went to the coat closet and got their coats.

"You're making a big mistake," Dad said to Trevor as the three of them were leaving.

"We'll take our chances," Trevor said. "Good night, all." He slammed the door behind him.

"Oh, dear," Mom said. "What a mess."

"I couldn't see slugging him," Dad said. "And he does have a right to see his kids."

"Connie didn't want him to see them this weekend," I said. "They had a big fight about it earlier."

"Why didn't you tell us that?" Mom asked.

"I didn't think it was my business," I said. "Melodie knew. She could have told you."

"You're right," Mom said. "Oh, well. They'll just have to work it out for themselves, I suppose."

"Come on, Mom," Mitch said. "Let's clear off the table."

"I'll help," Barry said.

"Boy," Steve whispered to me, as we returned to the dining room. "Things like that happen here often?"

"Never," I whispered back. But I had a sinking feeling they might be about to start.

Chapter

4

How about a soda?" Steve asked me after school on Monday. We can talk about the biology project."

"I'm worried about Melodie," I said. "I think I'd better go over to her house."

"Just because she missed a day of school?" Steve said. "You told me she's been missing a lot of school lately. Her father probably took her to Rome with him."

"You don't really think so?" I asked. "Connie would kill him if he did."

"I don't think Mr. Ashford cares about that," Steve said. "And I don't see why you care so much, so why not have a soda?"

"Soda is bad for your teeth," I said. "All that sugar. And you have no idea what Connie was like. She hung up on Mom and Dad three times Friday night before they could finally tell her the whole story. It was awful."

"So it was awful," Steve said. "And sodas cause cavities. How about milk, then, and you can tell me all about it."

"Come with me to Melodie's," I suggested instead.

"Are you crazy?" he said. "For all you know, she's dying of the plague and her mother is having hysteria attacks, and you want me to go over there with you? Her mother doesn't even know me. She'll probably have me arrested."

"Connie is okay, usually," I said. "But lately the strain's been getting to her. I could use the protection in case she's mad at me, too."

"Sorry," Steve said. "But my offer of milk and comfort still stands."

"Tomorrow after school," I said. "Before I have supper at Melodie's. But now I'd better see if Melodie is okay."

Steve scowled. "Promise about tomorrow?" he finally said.

"Absolutely promise," I said, and kissed him to seal the deal. Steve smiled at me and then wished me luck with my errand of mercy.

I felt like I was going to need all the luck I could find, and while I biked over to Melodie's house, I wondered if I was crazy to go visiting without being asked. There was a real possibility Melodie was still in the city with Trevor, in which case Connie would give it to me. Connie didn't usually scold me, but the couple of times she had I'd been scorched. My mom usually hollers for a moment, then looks upward and prays for a UFO to take her away. Connie is more theatrical.

Marta opened the door. I smiled, to show her I wasn't armed, and asked if Melodie was home.

Marta just nodded. Marta isn't one for conversation. At least she didn't frisk me. Instead, she pointed upstairs, and I figured Melodie was in her bedroom.

So I went up there, and sure enough there was Melodie. She wasn't crying this time. Instead, she was sitting on the bentwood rocker, rocking gently and looking determined.

"Hi," I whispered. "You okay?"

"Elaine!" she cried, and the next thing I knew she'd practically thrown herself into my arms. "How did you know I needed to see you?"

This was not Melodie-like behavior. I concentrated for a moment, and then I remembered who acted like that. Connie, of course. I wiggled out of the hug and said, "What's going on?"

"What isn't!" Melodie said, sounding a little more like herself. "Come on in. Sit down."

So I sat down under the canopy. "How was the weekend?" I asked, trying to sound light and chatty.

"Wonderful," Melodie said. "Awful. Crazy."

"You missed a geometry quiz," I said, still trying to figure out how to talk to her. Melodie sounded too much like Connie for my comfort. "A surprise quiz. It wasn't too hard, though."

"Geometry," Melodie said, and then she half laughed. It was definitely Connie's half-laugh. She used it whenever she was trying to cover her broken heart.

So I took the direct approach. "Cut the crap," I said. "You're acting really dumb, Melodie."

I guess that worked, because she started crying. "Close the door," she choked out, and I ran across the room and slammed the door shut. I stood there for a moment. Then I walked back to Melodie, and this time I hugged her. I even patted her on the back, the way Mom does me when I cry in front of her.

Melodie broke away from my hug and got a box of tissues, which she promptly started using. "I'm sorry," she muttered, after throwing the tissues away. "I don't even know who I am anymore."

"You're my best friend," I said firmly. "Your name is Melodie St. Clare Ashford, and you're a sophomore at Lassiter High School. And your parents may be crazy, but you're pretty sane."

"Thanks," she said. "Sometimes I wonder."

"Sometimes I wonder, too," I said. "About me, I mean. I want you to know Steve asked me out for a very exciting date of milk and biology projects, and I turned him down to find out what's going on here."

"You should have stayed with Steve," Melodie said. "But I'm glad you didn't."

"Then I'm glad, too," I said, even though that was at least partly a lie. "What happened? Why weren't you in school?"

"I couldn't face it," Melodie said. "Sit down, Elaine. You make me feel even weirder standing over me like that."

So I got back on the bed. I crossed my legs, after remembering to kick my shoes off, and prepared to listen.

But Melodie didn't say anything for a few minutes. I sat there and watched her rock and blow her nose. And then I started resenting her for keeping me from Steve, even though I knew she hadn't even asked me to come. But it can be awfully irritating just watching somebody rock.

"How was the movie?" I finally asked.

"Terrible," Melodie said. "I hate those stupid war movies."

"You do?" I asked. "I always thought you liked them."

"They're so dumb," she said. "Everybody knows how they're going to turn out. We won World War II, after all. And the biggest stars always live, and the character actors always get to have big death scenes, and the women get their blouses torn off. Big deal."

"Did Trevor buy you and Lissa new dresses?" I asked, hoping Melodie would whine less if we changed the subject.

"Pretty ones," Melodie said. "Lissa looked so cute in hers. And she did fall asleep right around ten, the way Daddy said. But they found a cot for her at the party, so she slept right through it."

"Did you meet any stars?" I asked. "New ones, I mean." Melodie had met just about every star in America. Even though she didn't get excited about it, I did.

"Just the same old dumb ones," she said. "Nobody you'd want to hear about."

I wanted to hear about all of them, but I shrugged my shoulders to show I was every bit as worldly as she. This time, I was behaving like Connie.

"You get home on Sunday?" I asked. Usually Melodie couldn't wait to tell me about her times with Trevor. Having her silent and rocking didn't make the situation any more pleasant.

"Mama sent Hans to pick us up at Daddy's," Melodie said. "I don't know how she figured out just the right time to do it, but he came while Daddy was

37

out. Daddy was out for only an hour on Sunday, but that was when Hans came. He swooped Lissa and me out of there, and shoved us in the car, and drove us home. Lissa cried the entire way. And it wasn't even like Mama was here when we got back. She was still in the city. Daddy called here every ten minutes until we got back, and then he insisted on talking to Miss Hardwick to make sure we were being supervised. The only person who was supervising us while Daddy was out was his valet, for heaven's sake, but he had to make sure Miss Hardwick was watching over us. And even when she swore we were okay, he insisted on talking to both of us."

"What's wrong with that?" I asked. When Dad called from Pittsburgh, he never insisted on anything except keeping the calls short.

"Lissa was still crying," Melodie said, looking at me like I was an idiot for not having known that. "And you can't imagine how upset Daddy got when he heard her."

I didn't really have the heart to tell Melodie that both her parents were crazy, so I just sat there and tried to think of something else to say. There didn't seem to be much, so we fell back into silence.

I guess that's why we could hear the doorbell ring, even though Melodie's door was closed. It rang a couple of times, and then somebody opened it. Even through the closed door, it was easy to hear Trevor's British accent.

"Oh, no," Melodie said. "It's Daddy."

"Is your mother around?" I asked, not sure what I wanted the answer to be.

Melodie nodded. "She's in the music room," she whispered. "What do you think I should do?"

"Nothing," I said. "Absolutely nothing. Let them scream it out for a while, and then everything will be okay."

"No, it won't," Melodie said. We could hear Marta's footsteps going up the stairs, and then the knock on the music room door. Connie must have been doing her voice exercises, because she sounded surprised when Marta told her Trevor was there. Surprised first, and then angry. We listened to the two pairs of feet clambering down the stairs. Melodie opened her door quietly, and we both sat down in the hallway, where we could hear everything.

"How dare you steal my daughters away from me like that!" Trevor shouted. Not even a hello, how are you. He got into the heavy stuff right away.

"I steal your daughters!" Connie screamed right back. "You went over to the Zuckermans' house and practically threatened the Zuckermans with physical violence, when all they were trying to do was give shelter to my two little girls."

"Maybe we shouldn't listen anymore," I whispered to Melodie, but there was no getting her away from there. She shook me off when I tried to get her back into her bedroom. But to be perfectly honest, I think we could have heard them even if we'd gone back in, closed the door, and plugged our ears with cotton balls. Trevor and Connie were both professional screamers.

"I don't know what sort of bilge the Zuckermans told you," Trevor said, "but I didn't threaten anyone.

39

I simply picked up my daughters for a weekend. A weekend we'd both agreed to quite a while ago, although you seem to have conveniently forgotten that."

"I didn't forget," she said. "I remembered all along. Even when it seemed like *you* had forgotten during your latest little escapade in Rome. Which starlet was it this time? Anita? Angelina Marcello?"

"I was there on business, as you well know," Trevor said in his most British accent. When Trevor gets angry enough, he sounds like the King of England. "And the moment I knew I'd be back in time I called you, and you said it was no longer convenient for you. As though your convenience could in any way affect my right to see my own daughters."

"I really wish you'd stop calling them that," Connie said. "They have names, in case you've forgotten."

"I remember," Trevor said. "I can remember a lot of things you'd probably prefer to forget."

"Oh, no," Melodie whispered. "They're really going to get ugly now."

I was amazed that she could tell the difference, but sure enough Trevor and Connie got into a real screaming match after that. They called each other all sorts of names and accused each other of things I don't think my parents ever even thought of. I could just barely see them through the spindles of the banister. As awful as it was to look at them, it was better than looking at Melodie. She was staring straight at her parents, as if they were on television.

Suddenly Connie slapped Trevor. I flinched when she did it, but I guess it didn't bother him too much because he laughed. It was a phony laugh, but it was better than his slugging her, which was what I was afraid would happen.

Before, when Connie and Trevor fought (which they did a lot even when they were happy), if one of them started laughing the other one would, too. They used to laugh a lot in those days, and Melodie laughed, too. Now Lissa was the only one who laughed, and it seemed she was doing it less and less.

"I want you out of here right now," Connie said when Trevor was through. "Do I have to call Hans, or will you leave on your own?"

"Call Hans," Trevor said. "But first I want you to understand something."

"Oh, I understand," Connie said. "I understand only too well what you're trying to do."

"Really?" Trevor said. "Would you care to explain it to me?"

"You're trying to destroy the precious relationship I have with my daughters," Connie said. "You spoil them with parties and presents, and then you make me out to be the heavy when I insist they eat right and go to school. I give them discipline and you tell them I'm some sort of villain. We can all see right through you."

"You give them discipline?" Trevor asked. "You were the one who said they could take next Monday off so you could see them in Boston. I assume you need to see them in Boston because you're too busy to see them in their own home."

"I am a working mother," Connie said. "But even with the many hours I have to put in to support myself and my children, I still see more of them than you ever dreamed of doing."

"I intend to remedy that," Trevor said. "And that is why I've come here today."

Melodie wasn't the only one listening. There wasn't another sound in the house. I had the awful feeling Lissa was all ears, too. I had all the proof I needed when suddenly the record player went on in her bedroom. Thank goodness for Miss Hardwick.

"We're all waiting," Connie said. "What is this grand announcement you have to make, Trevor?"

"I have an appointment with my attorneys tomorrow morning," Trevor said. "At which point I intend to introduce a formal request for custody of Melodie and Lissa."

"What?" Connie gasped. It wasn't a theatrical gasp, either.

"You heard me, my dear," Trevor said, all King of England again. "I'm suing for custody. And I have every reason to believe I'll win."

Connie shouted something, but I wasn't listening anymore. Instead, I turned to face Melodie. It was a good thing I did, too. Her face had gone so pale I was afraid she might faint.

"Miss Hardwick!" I shouted. "Come here, fast!"

"You see what you've done?" Connie screamed at Trevor. She raced up the stairs, and Trevor followed her. Miss Hardwick got to us first, though, and she helped get Melodie into her room and onto her bed. All the adults stood around, staring at Melodie.

"I've got to go now," I said, but nobody seemed to have heard me. They were all still staring. Whatever was going to happen next, though, I knew they'd be just as happy if I wasn't there to see it. So, feeling like a fool, I walked to the foot of the bed, picked up my shoes, and beat it out of there as fast as I could.

Chapter
5

When I got home Monday night, my parents looked a lot better to me than usual. Of course, Dad was in Pittsburgh, so it was hard to appreciate him, but Mom was around, and even her chatter about UFOs was more bearable than usual. There was nothing phony about it, at least. And she didn't go around referring to Mitch and Barry and me as "my children." She called us by our names and hollered at us when the table wasn't set for supper on time. Even that was okay. I'd rather set the table myself than deal with Hans and Marta.

Melodie wasn't in school the next day, but I couldn't blame her. If my parents had gone at it as viciously as hers, I would probably spend the next two years of my life hiding in my bedroom.

A couple of times during classes, I thought about Melodie and Lissa and how they were doing. I wouldn't have put it past Connie to have yanked them out of school and put them in some fancy boarding school, probably on a different continent. Someplace where Trevor couldn't find them. But I doubted that even Connie could arrange all that in twenty-four hours. Besides, Melodie would have called to let me know what was happening.

"How about our milk date?" Steve asked me, as we got out of school. The day was absolutely gorgeous, the sun shining and warming everything up. The first flowers of spring were blooming, and even our school looked pretty.

"Fine," I said. "Except let's go for a walk instead."

"Where do you want to walk?" he asked, linking his hand with mine.

"The park," I said. "Nobody ever walks in the park, and I think it gets lonely."

Steve laughed, but he knew what I meant. Most people in Morganville live in houses with big yards, and they don't need the park. So it just sits there, getting its grass trimmed and being ignored.

The park is only a few blocks from school, so it was a short walk. When we got there, we sat down on an empty bench.

"This is nice," Steve said, as we sat there holding hands and staring at the pattern of shadows the leaves were casting. "I'm glad you thought of it."

"I drink enough milk," I said. "One less glass won't kill me."

"Have any thoughts about the biology project?" he asked.

"Only that I don't want to do it," I said. "I don't like anything about biology, especially cutting up frogs."

"I kind of like it," he said. "I was thinking of becoming a doctor."

"Really?" I said. "You want to go through all that school?"

"If I have to," he said. "I guess I'd have to."

"They don't let people practice medicine with just a high school diploma," I said. "Even dental school takes a while."

"You want to be a dentist, like your mother?" Steve asked. "We could set up offices together."

"No, thank you," I said. "The offices sound nice, but I don't want to be a dentist. Mom spends her entire day staring at people's mouths. All she ever sees are teeth. And she doesn't even get to have conversations with her patients, because they have a mouthful of instruments. Sometimes she tells them about UFOs, but they don't get to tell her anything back. What's the fun of that?"

"None, I guess," Steve said. "So what do you want to do?"

"I know what I don't want to do," I said. "I don't want to be a doctor or a dentist or a computer chips executive. I don't want to be the mother of twins or a UFO nut or have anything to do with show business. What does that leave me?"

"Plenty," Steve said. "What's this about show business, though? I thought you thought Melodie's parents were terrific."

"I was wrong," I said, and told him a little bit about what had happened the day before. I didn't want to be indiscreet, but I'd been going crazy not telling people. "They were so awful," I concluded. "And so theatrical. I don't even think they meant half the things they said."

"No wonder Melodie's so weird," Steve said.

"Melodie isn't the least bit weird," I said. "Be-

46

sides, I thought doctors were supposed to be full of compassion."

"I am full of compassion," Steve replied. "I feel sorry for Melodie for being so weird."

I punched him in the arm. Not hard, though, and since we were all alone in the park, Steve took that to mean I wanted him to kiss me. He was right, too.

"We've got to do this more often," he said. "This park is very romantic."

"I thought it was me," I said.

"You definitely help," he said, and we kissed again. I really liked the feel of his face next to mine, and our lips touching. It made me feel very close to Steve. I wondered if Trevor and Connie had ever felt close, and that made me feel bad, so I broke away.

"What is it?" Steve asked.

"Nothing," I said, not wanting to tell him what I was thinking. It was really very dumb. Trevor and Connie had probably felt a good deal closer at some point during their marriage, and what good had it done them? Feeling close for a moment, or a day, or even a year didn't mean you were going to stay close forever.

"I know what you need," Steve said.

"Tell me," I said. I was starting to feel almost weepy, and that didn't seem fair. It wasn't my parents who were going crazy.

"You need some of my mother's cookies," Steve said. "I know for a fact that she baked chocolate chip cookies today."

"Chocolate chips are my favorite," I said, feeling cheerier already.

"Chocolate chips are everybody's favorite," Steve said.

"She won't mind if I come over?" I asked.

"She'll love it," Steve said. "Come on, it won't take long."

So we got up and walked slowly through the park. And when we got to Steve's house, we went in through the kitchen, where, sure enough, his mother was standing over a plate stacked with freshly baked cookies.

"Perfect timing," she said. "Hello, Elaine, dear. It's so nice to see you again."

Mrs. Miller had the most wonderful manners. Nothing fancy, just good old-fashioned affectionate. She even kissed me on the cheek, before thrusting a cookie into my hand.

"These cookies are wonderful," I said, eating mine in three blissful bites. "Mrs. Miller, you're the best baker in the world."

"In the universe," Steve said. "The way Elaine's mother thinks, that means there's plenty of competition."

"I've been meaning to thank your mother for having Steve over for dinner Friday night," Mrs. Miller said. "He told me what a fine time he had."

"We all had a good time," I said, choosing to forget about Trevor's little scene.

"I have a wonderful idea," Mrs. Miller said. "Elaine, darling, why don't you stay for supper?"

"Oh, I couldn't," I said. "Tuesdays I always have supper with my friend Melodie."

"Elaine's social calendar always starts with Melodie," Steve said, giving me a look.

"I'm sure she won't mind if you skip one Tuesday," Mrs. Miller said. "Why don't you call her and ask?"

Dinner with Steve and his parents sounded a whole lot cheerier than supper with a mournful Melodie and Lissa. And what was one Tuesday after we'd shared thousands of them? So I walked over to the phone and dialed Melodie's number. Miss Hardwick answered.

"Hi," I said. "Is Melodie around?"

"Melodie's washing her hair, Elaine," Miss Hardwick said. "Can she call you back in a few minutes?"

"No, that isn't necessary," I said, feeling a great sense of relief. "Just tell her I won't be over for supper tonight, okay?"

"Is everything all right?" Miss Hardwick asked.

"Oh, sure," I said. "It's just that something's come up. I'll see Melodie in school tomorrow." I hung up before I had to explain any further.

"Am I still invited?" I asked Mrs. Miller as I hung up.

"You certainly are," she said. "We're having lamb chops. I hope you like them."

"I love them," I said.

"You know, if you always have dinner with your friend, maybe you should call your mother and tell her you'll be here instead," Mrs. Miller said. "Just in case they need to reach you."

I didn't think it was necessary, but it was one of those suggestions mothers make that are hard to argue with. So I went back to the phone and called home. I got Barry and told him what was happening.

"Changing your Tuesday plans?" he said. "Well, we aren't changing ours. Mom's going to her meeting tonight, and Dad won't be home for supper. Mitch and I are going out for pizza."

So I hung up and took another couple of cookies to tide me over until suppertime.

Steve and I got our books and went to the living room, where we half studied, half kissed. It didn't seem right to more than half kiss, with his mother in the kitchen.

"This is so nice of your mother," I told him during a study-and-kiss break. We had those pretty frequently, since it's hard to talk when you're studying or kissing. Married students probably never talk.

"She's okay," Steve said. "She worries sometimes that you don't approve of all her baking."

"Approve?" I said. "I think it's wonderful."

"You know," he said, "your mother and all those cavities."

"You can get pretty tired of cheddar cheese," I said. "And even my mother loves chocolate chip cookies."

"See if you can work that into tonight's conversation," Steve said, and then the kissing break ended, and we kissed some more. Then the study break ended, and we got back to work, which wasn't nearly as much fun.

"Hi, Elaine," Dr. Miller said, when he got home from work. "It's nice to see you."

"Mom invited her to stay for supper," Steve said. "Hi, Dad."

"Hi, son," Dr. Miller said. "That's nice, Elaine. Supper smells delicious."

"Lamb chops," Steve said.

"Great," Dr. Miller said, and wandered off to the

kitchen, probably to tell his wife how good everything smelled and steal a cookie. None of the Millers had a weight problem, but food seemed awfully important to them. I thought it was wonderful that they had something they all enjoyed together. My family seemed to be divided into units that got along fine but didn't have many things to enjoy together.

"You're not thinking about biology," Steve said.

"I was thinking about how nice your family is," I replied.

"I like them," he said. "I miss Debbie, though."

Debbie was Steve's older sister. She was a freshman in college. Mitch and Barry were going to go to college next year, but I couldn't picture missing them.

"Supper's ready," Mrs. Miller called, and we went to the kitchen, where she'd set the table. Dr. Miller was right. Everything did smell wonderful. It tasted even better. There were lamb chops and broccoli and wild rice, and, in my honor, Mrs. Miller had baked biscuits, too. All from scratch. My parents' idea of scratch is to open the plastic bag the frozen vegetables come in.

So I ate a lot, which was a good thing, since Mrs. Miller kept telling me to eat some more. I tried to remember what Debbie looked like, and it came to me that she was a little chunky. Who could blame her?

During supper Dr. and Mrs. Miller made a point of asking me a lot of questions, like how my parents were and how things were going with school. Friendly questions. And Dr. Miller discussed how his workday had gone. He wasn't gruesome about it; he just told us about the different sick animals and what their owners were like. Being a veterinarian was obviously a lot more interesting than being a computer chips executive and more pleasant than being a dentist. But if I couldn't even cut up a frog, I didn't think it was the right line of work for me.

Whenever Mrs. Miller talked, except when she told all of us to eat more, it was to discuss her husband's day, and Steve's and mine. But then she told us a little about what had happened to her. She did volunteer work at the hospital, so her stories were interesting, too.

I loved it. No talk about software versus hardware and other civilizations and baseball. Just interesting anecdotes.

Dessert was chocolate chip cookies and homemade vanilla ice cream. That was when I knew I'd died and gone to heaven. If my mother ever made ice cream, it would probably be cheddar-cheese-flavored. I ate more than my share and then had a little more. If the Millers were my parents, I'd weigh two hundred pounds. But, boy, I'd be happy.

"I'll do the dishes," I offered. It was the least I could do, having eaten them out of house and home.

"Don't be silly," Mrs. Miller said. "You're a guest."

"Can't I do something?" I asked.

"You can stay and keep me company," she said. "You can tell me more about that fascinating mother of yours. I always marvel at how she manages a full-time practice and raises such lovely children. Not to mention her many interests."

So Steve and his father went into the living room, and I tried to explain to Mrs. Miller Mom's various timesaving techniques, which basically consisted of not worrying if the house was clean or if we were well fed. Only I wasn't quite that blunt.

"I wish I could be that way," Mrs. Miller said. "People like your mother always get so much more accomplished than I ever will."

"You've accomplished a lot," I said, taking one last cookie to prove it.

She finished drying the dishes and turned to me. "I'm a dying breed," she said. "The full-time housewife. You might call me a dinosaur."

"I think it's great," I said.

"Would you want your mother to be one?" she asked. "Now, be honest, Elaine."

The thought of having my mother around all the time with nothing to keep her mind off of UFOs except keeping the house clean and cooking was so awful my face immediately dropped. Mrs. Miller saw it.

"You see," she said. "But that's all right. We all do what we have to do, and I guess I was just born to be a housewife."

So I thought some then about being a housewife for a career. Only I'm not a very good cook, and to become one, I'd probably get fat from practicing. And nothing could make me a good housecleaner. Another career choice down the drain.

"It's time for you to go home," Mrs. Miller said, taking off her apron. "It is a school night, after all."

"That's right," I said. "I'll get my books, and say good night, and go home."

"Ask my husband to drive you," she said. "If he's too tired, I will."

But Dr. Miller agreed to, so he and Steve took me

back. When we got there, all the lights were off. I explained to them that everybody was out, but Steve insisted on walking me to the door to make sure everything was all right before they left. Everything was, so they left immediately, but I liked their thoughtfulness.

I'd just dumped my books on the sofa and was hanging up my jacket when the phone rang. I ran to the kitchen and got it.

"Elaine? Is that you? Are you all right?"

"Sure I am," I said. "Why, Melodie? Why shouldn't I be?"

"You always have supper here on Tuesday," she said. "I've been frantic. I've been calling every five minutes, and nobody's answered and I thought something horrible must have happened, an accident or something. I've been going crazy. I almost called the police."

"Oh, Melodie," I said. "I gave Miss Hardwick the message. Didn't she tell you I called?"

"She told me," Melodie said. "But she said you didn't give a reason why you wouldn't be having supper here."

"I was at Steve's," I said. "Steve's mother practically insisted I have supper there, and you weren't in school today, so I figured you probably weren't feeling too well, anyway. It never occurred to me you'd get upset over it."

"Well, I did," she said.

"Well, you shouldn't have," I said. "It wasn't as if I didn't call."

"Oh, you called all right," Melodie said, and I could

54

hear the bitterness in her voice. "You called and left a cowardly little message. You weren't even honest enough to tell me you'd rather have dinner with your precious Steve than see me, when you know we always have dinner together Tuesdays."

"Maybe it's time for a change, then," I said. "You've been pretty tiresome lately."

By the time I realized what a rotten thing that was to say, Melodie had slammed the phone down.

I dialed her number right away, but Miss Hardwick answered and said Melodie didn't feel like talking anymore.

I felt bad for Melodie, but I was angry, too. Where was it written that I had to have dinner with her every Tuesday? Especially since every time I saw her lately, it seemed like a bomb went off at my feet.

Being a friend was supposed to mean having fun. Where had the fun gone with Melodie?

Chapter

6

S he blames you?" Steve asked me before school the next day. "Like it was your fault?"

"Well, it was, I guess," I said. Melodie was back at school, but she was standing by herself in the schoolyard. She looked awful, and it was all I could do not to go up to her and apologize, but I didn't. Partly because I didn't want to, and partly because I was scared of what Melodie would say. She had a "Hands Off" sign on her, and I figured that applied to me as much as to the rest of the world.

"She doesn't own you," Steve said. "There's no law saying you have to have supper at her house every Tuesday."

"I know," I said. "But I always do."

"Some habits are made to be broken," he said. "Besides, didn't you have a good time at my house?"

"I had a wonderful time," I said, smiling at the memory. "Your parents couldn't have been nicer."

"They like you, too," he said, and he put his hand on mine. Hugging and kissing were not approved of in the Lassiter High schoolyard, but handholding was safe. "Mom asked when we could expect to see you again."

"I don't want to wear out my welcome," I said. I vaguely remembered hearing my mother say that once.

"That would be impossible," Steve said, and smiled. I smiled back. So what if Melodie was furious at me and would probably never speak to me again. I had Steve, which was more than she'd ever have. Especially if she kept on being so melodramatic. Just like her parents.

I tried my hardest not to think about Melodie for the rest of the day, but that wasn't easy, since we had a lot of classes together. And people were constantly asking me about her.

"Has Melodie been sick?" someone asked. "Is that why she's been missing so much school?"

"I don't know," I said. "You'll have to ask her."

"What's going on with Melodie?" someone else asked. "She's looked like she's about to scream all day long."

"I don't have the slightest idea," I said. "You'll have to ask Melodie."

And, finally: "Melodie's in the girls' room, crying. Do you think you should do something about it?"

"What should I do?" I asked. "She can blow her own nose."

But I felt awful as soon as the words had left my mouth. Maybe I should go to the girls' room to see if I could help. Maybe she was crying because of our fight, although I doubted that. More likely, she was doing it to get me to apologize. And I wasn't going to apologize. Not then. Not ever. I was entitled to a life of my own, a fun life with Steve and his parents, who were sane and healthy and normal.

I walked home from school alone that day and thought about it some more. Melodie, I decided, was determined to feel sorry for herself, no matter what. After all, what was the problem? Just that both parents wanted her and Lissa. Actually, that was kind of nice. Lots of fathers walk out and never think about their kids again. I knew kids at school who hardly ever heard from their fathers after the divorce was final; they remarried and settled in with a new family and didn't care about the old one. That would be awful. Having Trevor care so much that he was willing to fight for Melodie and Lissa was reassuring. It would be to me, if I were Melodie.

And Connie was willing to fight, too. She might be wrong, but it was natural that she saw Trevor as a bad influence. And, even if she didn't, she wouldn't want to lose custody. She was used to having Melodie and Lissa around. She might not see all that much of them, but she loved them and wanted to watch them grow up.

If my parents ever got divorced, I couldn't see them making any sort of fuss over me. I didn't think it would be a you-take-her, no-you-take-her situation. They both love me. But Dad has those trips to Pittsburgh, and Mom has her practice; and if one of them volunteered to keep me around, the other one would probably be just as happy. Mitch and Barry, I figured, would just get custody of each other.

Then I started thinking about what it would be like

if my parents did split up and have a custody fight, and I had to testify. It sounded exciting. I'd get up on the witness stand, and I'd look pathetic and pretty. My skin would be completely clear, and all my cowlicks would have disappeared. I'd be wearing something black and stark and I'd be carrying a handkerchief, which I'd twist in my hands during moments of stress. My lip would quiver, too, but except for one perfect tear I'd somehow get to roll down my right cheek, I'd be in complete control.

The only problem with the fantasy was that I couldn't see where it could possibly go. Suppose the lawyers tried to get me to shred my parents into little pieces. What could I possibly say? They were both so boring. There would be no way the judge could make up his mind. He'd probably split me right in half.

Then I wondered if maybe that was what would happen to Melodie and Lissa. Maybe they'd live with Connie half the year and Trevor the other half. Where would they go to school? Or maybe Connie would get one of them and Trevor would get the other. Melodie was more likely to go to Trevor, since she was older, and his bad influence wouldn't be so bad on her. If Melodie was in New York, when would I ever see her? Trevor might put her in some European boarding school so he could see her when he was abroad. He might even move them both back to England so he could become Sir Trevor Ashford.

I didn't want to lose Melodie forever. It was one thing to be mad at her. It was quite another to have her live three thousand miles away, locked up in some Swiss school, doing nothing but skiing.

Melodie loved skiing. She wouldn't mind. She'd be happy to go to Switzerland and make all new friends and lead a glamorous life. She had glamorous parents, after all, and that was what she'd been brought up to expect. She'd probably marry a prince or become a movie star or a diplomat. Something spectacular. While I stayed in Morganville and went into computer chips. Or became a dentist. Or something even worse, although I couldn't imagine what that might be.

I got myself so upset by the time I got home that even the twins noticed. "What is it, Elaine?" Mitch asked. "You look like you just lost your best friend."

"I did," I said, and started to cry. Mitch and Barry stared at each other, and then Barry put his arms around me. He wasn't used to it and it was a little awkward, but it felt good, anyway.

I didn't cry for very long, partly because I felt I had an obligation to Barry not to. Mitch got a box of tissues and handed them to me. I didn't use more than two or three, and then I heaved a couple of times.

"Wash your face with cold water," Mitch said. "That's what Mom always says to do."

So I did, and I felt better after that. I wasn't sure Mitch and Barry would still be waiting for me when I got out of the bathroom, but they were just where I'd left them. They were talking to each other, and I got the feeling it was about me. I was sure that was the first time they'd ever talked about me. So I smiled.

"Problems with Melodie?" Barry asked, as I sat down in the living room.

"She's mad at me about last night," I said.

"She'll get over that," Mitch said. "That's not the kind of thing that breaks up a friendship."

"I know," I said. "But things are so crazy in her life right now, I just don't know what's going to happen. Trevor is threatening to sue for custody."

"I thought he might," Barry said. "The way he was acting Friday night, I didn't think he was going to stick to Connie's rules."

"But if he wins, I don't know what will happen to Melodie," I said. "Trevor could take her to live anywhere, and I'd never see her again."

"I don't think Trevor will win," Mitch said. "Not unless Melodie would really much rather live with him than with Connie. Do you think that's true?"

I thought about it. Melodie and Connie didn't get along all the time, but for the most part things were good between them. And I knew Melodie wouldn't want to be parted from Lissa. And since I'd decided that Connie would be awarded custody of Lissa no matter what, I felt better. "Melodie loves Trevor," I said. "But she loves Connie, too. She wants to be able to see both of them."

"I don't blame her," Barry said. "I'd hate it if Mom and Dad broke up and we had to pick one parent to live with."

"Even if they did, they wouldn't fight about it the way Trevor and Connie did," I said. "Connie slapped Trevor and they called each other awful names Monday. It was horrible."

"No wonder you didn't want to go over there Tuesday," Mitch said.

"I didn't *not* want to go," I said. "But Steve was so insistent."

61

"And you couldn't have convinced him to wait until Wednesday?" Barry asked.

"Maybe I was glad for the excuse," I admitted.

"Maybe," Mitch said, but he smiled at me.

"Do you think I should apologize to Melodie?" I asked. I could hardly believe I was asking the twins for advice, or that they were talking with me about my problems. It was what having big brothers was supposed to be like.

"If you really don't think you were wrong, you shouldn't apologize," Mitch said. "But you've got to remember, Melodie is very upset about what's going on. She needs her friends. She needs them more than she ever has before. She must be terrified of losing everything. Her home and her parents and maybe even Lissa. The last thing she needs is to worry that she's going to lose you, too."

"I know you're right," I said. "But she's been so grim lately. Melodie used to be so much fun, and now all she does is stay home from school and feel sorry for herself."

"You never feel sorry for yourself?" Barry said. "You're not feeling sorry for yourself right now?"

I knew he was teasing, but it didn't bother me. It was his way of making a point.

"Okay," I grumbled. "I'll call. I'll apologize. I'll be understanding. But she'd better not keep acting like this. I don't know how much of it I can take."

"Things will get better," Mitch said. "And Melodie will appreciate having a friend who cares so much."

I wasn't sure whether I was supposed to thank them. For a moment I thought about telling them that I loved them, but that seemed much too embarrassing to do. Still, I felt I ought to say something.

"How come you guys know so much?" I finally said. It wasn't at all what I wanted to say, and it sounded awful; but having said it, I didn't know how I could improve it.

"We're older," Barry said.

"And smarter," Mitch said.

"And better-looking," Barry said.

So then they were just the dumb old twins again, and we all felt comfortable. I never thought I'd be happy to hear them being mean, but I guess they felt awkward, too, about paying attention to me. I stuck my tongue out at them and went to the kitchen to call Melodie and make up.

I started dialing the number, and then I hung up. I didn't have the slightest idea what to say. I knew I didn't want to start out apologizing. I wasn't angry anymore, but I didn't feel guilty about not having supper with her, either. After all, Melodie had to understand me, too, occasionally.

But I couldn't just casually say, "Hi," and act like nothing had happened. Not the way Melodie had been behaving all day.

I finally decided I'd say, "I'm sorry, Melodie," without saying what I was sorry about. I'd know I was sorry that her parents were being so rotten and her life was such misery, but she'd think I meant I was sorry I'd skipped supper the night before. That seemed the safest approach.

So I dialed Melodie's number. But instead of hearing her pick up, I got a recorded announcement.

"The number you have dialed has been changed or disconnected. Please ask the operator for further assistance."

I didn't believe it, so I dialed again. I got the same recording.

My immediate thought was that Trevor had stolen Melodie and Lissa, and Connie had already had the number disconnected. Only then I calmed down and realized Melodie had been in school that day. Maybe there was just something the matter with the telephone.

So then I dialed Connie's number. I knew it from the years before Melodie had been given her own phone. I girded myself for a quick conversation with Hans or Marta, but instead I got the same recording.

This time I knew better than to dial again. I also knew better than to worry for very long that Connie had taken the girls and moved away. Melodie was in school that afternoon. And it was a matinee day. An A-bomb wouldn't keep Connie away from the theater on a Wednesday.

So I called the operator for further assistance. "May I have the number for Melodie Ashford?" I asked. "It's a new number."

The operator took a moment and then said, "I'm sorry, that number is unlisted."

"Do you have one for Constance King, then?" I asked.

Same brief silence. Same brief answer. It was unlisted.

"Please," I said. "Melodie is my best friend and I have to get through to her. Constance King is her mother. Can't you please give me her number?"

"I'm sorry," the operator said, but she didn't sound sorry at all. "That's against company policy."

My mother always says you can't fight with the phone company, so I didn't try. Instead, I hung up and wondered what to do. I didn't want to bike over to Melodie's, but if that was what was necessary, then I'd do it. I still had my jacket on, so I figured I'd probably intended to do that all along.

Just as I was getting my bag and deciding to let Mitch and Barry know where I was going and how they wouldn't be able to call me, the phone rang. I picked it up on the first ring.

"Elaine? It's Melodie."

"Thank God," I said. "Are you okay? Your number's been changed and it's unlisted and the operator wouldn't give it to me. I practically begged."

"I know," she said. "Mama had the numbers changed today so Daddy won't be able to get through to us."

"But that's terrible," I said. "What if he needs to talk to you?"

"I don't know," she said. "I don't know anything anymore. Elaine, things are so awful here. I don't know how much longer I'm going to be able to take it."

And that was when I knew Melodie didn't want to hear me say, "I'm sorry." She didn't care about apologies.

"It's okay," I said instead. "It'll be okay. Your parents are acting crazy now, but they'll get over it. I promise. Things will get better."

I could hear her crying on the other end, and I thought about her crying in the girls' room and felt awful. So I did what I could. "It'll be okay," I murmured over and over. "Don't worry, Melodie. It'll be okay. I promise."

I said it for as long as it took her to stop crying.

Chapter

7

W ant to come shopping with me?" Melodie asked me after school on Thursday. She sounded almost shy.

"I'd love to," I said. "What are we shopping for?"

"Lissa's birthday is in a couple of weeks," Melodie said, and we started walking toward the shopping mall. "With everything that's been going on, I haven't even thought about what to get her."

"I can't believe she'll actually be eight," I said. "I remember when she was born."

"I stayed at your house that night," Melodie said. "It was the first time I ever did."

"We'd just gotten to be friends," I said. "You didn't want sleep at all that night. You kept slipping over to the telephone, waiting for it to ring."

"The twins teased me so much," Melodie said. "And I decided I wanted anything, just as long as it wasn't a brother."

"I told you you didn't want a brother," I said. "That was the first thing I ever really said to you. Boy, was I happy when you had a baby sister."

"I was so happy then," Melodie said. "Listen to me. I'm fifteen years old, and I'm going around reminiscing about the good old days."

"Well, these days aren't so good," I said. "I guess it's natural."

"These days are awful," she said. I waited for her to continue. Melodie laughed. "You look so tragic," she said. "Have I been that awful lately?"

I nodded.

"Poor Elaine," she said. "I know it isn't your problem."

"It is, too," I said. "If you're my best friend then it's my problem, too. I don't like seeing you so unhappy."

"Today I'll be happy," she promised. "Shopping for Lissa always makes me happy."

"Mom's birthday is coming up next month, too," I said. "I should look for something for her while I'm here."

"I got her a book by Carl Sagan," Melodie said. "Doris has been so nice to me lately, I want to get her something. And Sagan believes in life in outer space, too, so I figured she'd like the book."

"I don't believe you already have a present for my mother," I said. "I haven't gotten anything for Lissa yet."

"I saw the book and it made me think of her," Melodie said. "It's just a paperback. It's no big deal."

"Maybe I'll get her a hardback of the same book," I said. "Then she'll know which one of us loves her more."

Melodie laughed again. I couldn't remember the

last time I'd heard her laugh twice in a minute. Maybe that was my fault. I might not have been as funny as usual with Melodie. You never knew when humor would be welcome, though.

"Let's start with the toy shop," Melodie said when we got to the mall. "And then if there's nothing there, we'll get ice cream sundaes."

"What if there is something there?" I asked.

"We'll get sundaes, anyway," she said. "If your teeth can stand the corruption."

"Do you know Mom gave me a traveling toothbrush and a little container of toothpaste?" I asked, trying not to sound shrill. "For me to use whenever I visit Steve's mother."

Melodie giggled. "That'll keep your teeth clean," she said. "But what about the calories in all the stuff you keep telling me about?"

"The calories are worth it," I said. "Besides, Mom doesn't worry about calories. Teeth always stay the same weight."

I didn't hang out much in the toy shop, since I'd outgrown most of the stuff there, except for the board games, which weren't my favorites, and the computerized games, which Dad always said we shouldn't buy retail since he could get them for us cheaper. He didn't get them for us but he kept saying he could, and that was enough to keep me from buying them. I couldn't afford them, anyway, so it was a good thing I didn't want them.

Melodie walked over to the doll section, and I followed her. There certainly was no shortage of dolls.

"Lissa would like that one," I said, pointing to a

69

bride doll. It was wearing a beautiful white gown and had a long lace veil over thick black hair.

Melodie picked up the doll and looked at the price tag. "It's a lot of money," she said.

"Can't you afford it?" I asked. Money was never one of Melodie's problems.

"Sure I can," she said. "But I don't know whether I should get Lissa anything so fancy. Lately Daddy and Mama have been into competitive gift-giving, and they've gotten pretty extravagant."

"I should have such problems," I said.

"Out of everything that's been going on, that's been the least of it," Melodie said. "But they're both spoiling Lissa rotten. Miss Hardwick is getting worried."

"She told you that?" I asked.

"Not in so many words," Melodie said, putting the doll back on the shelf. "But I can tell."

"So do you think you should get something cheap for Lissa?" I asked. "They have plenty of cheap stuff up front."

"I don't want to get Lissa something cheap, either," Melodie said. "Then she might decide I don't love her. Just something medium-priced."

"Maybe a stuffed animal," I said. "Lissa loves stuffed animals."

"That's an idea," Melodie said, and we walked over to that section.

I still had a fondness for stuffed animals; they were all so cute. We didn't have any pets because the twins were allergic to anything with hair. I probably was allergic, too, but it was irritating never having the chance to find out. I picked up a lavender bunny rabbit and showed it to Melodie. "This is just the right color for Lissa's bedroom," I said.

"If we get to stay there," she said, almost absently, while she looked at the price tag.

"What do you mean?" I asked. "Of course you'll stay there. Where else would you go?"

"Who knows?" she said with a shrug. "Daddy might win. Or maybe Mama's parents will get into the act. Or even Penelope. Kids do get awarded to their grandparents. I saw that on a soap opera once."

"Soap operas aren't real life," I said. "Besides, the problem isn't that neither of your parents wants you. You're more likely just to get split up."

Melodie whirled around to face me. She looked stricken. "Do you really think so?" she asked. "Did your parents say that?"

"Melodie, I'm sorry," I said. "I don't know what's going to happen to you."

"Did your parents say they thought we'd get split up?" Melodie asked. "And if they did, what did they mean? One of us would go to Daddy, and the other to Mama? Do they think that?"

"Dad's been in Pittsburgh all week," I said. "And I haven't talked to Mom about it, so as far as I know they don't have any opinion. All I meant was that maybe you'd spend the school year with Connie and the summers with Trevor."

"Or vice versa," Melodie said. "Or maybe we'll spend one week with Mama and one week with Daddy. We could do that if Mama moves to New York. Or weeks with one of them and weekends with the other. Or one night with one and one night with the other. Or alternate Christmases. Or alternate years."

"It would be easier for you to see your father if you moved to New York," I admitted reluctantly. "You'd probably see more of your mother, too."

Melodie put the stuffed rabbit back on the shelf. "Nothing too color-coordinated," she said. "Maybe just a standard color teddy bear." She picked one up and looked it over carefully.

"I don't want you to move," I said. I didn't have the slightest idea what I was supposed to say, but at least that was the truth.

"I don't want to move, either," Melodie said. "My friends are all here. Your family. I don't know what I'd do without your family."

"Take them, they're yours," I said.

"Don't joke about that," Melodie said fiercely. "You don't know how terrific your parents are."

"They're okay, but they're not exactly perfect."

"No family is exactly perfect," Melodie said. "What do you want? The kind of family they have on TV? With the perfect daddy and the perfect mommy and the two perfect kids?"

"They don't have those families on TV anymore," I said. "Just on reruns. Nowadays all the families on TV are divorced and miserable just like in the real world."

"Then you should really know how lucky you are," she said. "Your parents love each other and they love you and the twins. They're always there for you. You're crazy if you don't know how rare that is."

I wanted to say I wanted parents like Steve had,

sane and homey, but that seemed disloyal. And if Melodie thought *my* parents were so great, she'd probably die if she learned how terrific Steve's parents were. So I kept my mouth shut.

"I'm not going to find anything today," Melodie said. "Nothing looks right."

"You don't have to get something here," I said. "We could try someplace else."

"Not today," she said. "You want to look for something for your mother?"

"After we get our sundaes," I said, and then as I walked through the aisles, I found something. "This is it," I called to Melodie. "The perfect gift for Mom."

Melodie took the box from my hand. "BUILD YOUR OWN UFO," she read from the box. "Elaine, this is wonderful."

"Maybe not," I said. "Sometimes Mom gets touchy if she thinks we're making fun of her UFOs."

"But this really is great," Melodie said, checking out the box. "It looks just like all those UFO pictures Doris shows us all the time."

"Mom's good at putting things together," I said, taking the box from Melodie. "She says it's all that practice from filling teeth."

"I think you should get it," Melodie said. "It's absolutely perfect."

I looked at the box again. It was awfully expensive for a gift Mom might hate. I put it back on the shelf. "Maybe I'll hint to her about it," I said. "Mention that I saw it, and if she sounds interested, I'll get it for her."

"That's a good idea," Melodie said. "The sundaes are on me."

"That's not necessary," I said.

"I insist," she said. "I've been such a grouch lately, I owe you some hot fudge."

I never turn down persuasive arguments. We went to the ice cream parlor and ordered our sundaes. And while we ate them we talked about school, and the kids there, and Steve. Good stuff. Normal stuff. The stuff we used to talk about all the time. Melodie even listened politely when I told her how wonderful Steve was. It made me wish she had a boyfriend to brag to me about.

But if she had a boyfriend and she did have to leave, he'd be one more person it would hurt Melodie to leave behind. So even though I was scared I might be making a mistake, I said, "Melodie, no matter what, no matter where you live, you'll always be my best friend. Even if you live someplace really far away, I'll find a way of seeing you. There's always the phone. And that box of stationery your mother gave me for my birthday last year."

"You still haven't used that?" Melodie asked.

"I haven't had a reason to," I said. "Who was I supposed to write to?"

"I don't know," Melodie said. "But I hope I won't be the first person to get a letter from you."

"I hope so, too," I said. "But it'll be okay if you are."

Melodie looked down at her sundae. "I guess I'd be moving away in a couple of years, anyway," she said. "To go to college."

"Sure," I said. "And your mother would probably be moving back to New York then."

"And I could see you weekends," she said. "Even if I had to spend them with Daddy or Mama—I mean if it was arranged so that I couldn't get out of it—you could still come to the city. We could have such a good time in New York together. We could go to movies and museums and just stay up all night talking."

I knew that meant I wouldn't be able to see as much of Steve. And even though the thought made me sad, eventually I'd go into the city less and less frequently. So I just nodded. "It would be great," I said. "Not that I want you to go away. But it'll be okay if you have to."

"Do you think I should tell Mama my idea?" she asked. "Or Daddy?"

"Not yet," I said. "Besides, maybe they'll think of it all by themselves."

"The only thing they're thinking of these days is how to hurt each other," Melodie said, putting down change for a tip.

"That won't last," I said. "After a while they're bound not to hate each other so much."

"I hope so," Melodie said, and we got up. She paid the cashier, and we walked out to the mall. "If you come to my house Hans can give you a lift home," she said.

That seemed like a good idea, even though going to Melodie's house reminded me a lot of going into one of her father's movies. Your basic World War II motif.

"I still think you should get your mother that UFO model," Melodie said as we walked to her house. "She could display it in her office when she's finished."

"I'd kill her if she did," I said. "Do you know what

it's like when the other kids tell me all about how she drilled their teeth talking about UFOs? It's so embarrassing."

"You embarrass too easily," Melodie said, but she didn't sound mean about it. "Maybe instead of getting Lissa something, I should do something with her for her birthday. Take her someplace special."

"That's a great idea," I said. "We could all go roller skating. Lissa loves doing that, and Miss Hardwick really hates it."

"Roller skating and then someplace really dumpy for supper," Melodie said. "Whenever Daddy or Mama take her out for dinner, it's always a fancy restaurant. Lissa would love to get some junky fast food."

"And then maybe a tiny present," I said. "A Frisbee, maybe. So she'll have something to unwrap."

"I think that sounds perfect," Melodie said. "Even if Daddy and Mama do something special for Lissa's birthday, it won't be anything dumb and fun. Daddy'll probably get a copy of some Disney movie and have Lissa invite some friends over to see it, and then there'll be cake. And Mama will probably arrange for Lissa to go to the matinee of something like *Annie* and then go backstage to meet the actors. And then birthday cake. With split-up parents, you get a lot of birthday cake."

"You can't have too much for me," I said. "You know, Melodie, the stuff you just said your parents would do sounds great."

"It is great, I guess," Melodie said. "But Lissa would prefer roller skating and hamburgers."

There was no accounting for taste. But then I remembered what I liked to do when I was eight, and it was no great shakes. Although even at that age I would have liked all the birthday cake.

"Mom used to go crazy trying to make a fuss over each of the twins on their birthday," I said, as we approached Melodie's house. "So they'd feel individual, even though they had the exact same birthday and people were always buying one present for the two of them."

"I remember her at their bar mitzvah party," Melodie said. "Going through all the gifts for Mitch and for Barry and for both Mitch and Barry. She was terrified that the Mitch pile would be bigger than the Barry pile and vice versa."

"That's your second vice versa today," I said. "I've been keeping count."

"I'm glad to see you can count to two," Melodie said, and we both laughed. We were still laughing as she let herself into the house. She went to put away her books and jacket, but I decided to keep mine in case Hans drove me home immediately.

While she was at the closet the phone rang. I automatically answered it.

"King residence," I said. That always sounded so much classier than "Zuckerman residence."

"Is Melodie Ashford there?" the voice on the other end asked.

"Who's calling, please?" I asked.

"A friend of her father's," the voice said.

"One minute, please," I said, and handed the phone to Melodie, who had joined me. "He says he's a friend of your father's," I whispered.

"Hello?" Melodie said, and then she was silent for a moment. I could see how upset she was getting. Then she took a deep breath, and when she spoke again it was with a thick British accent, the kind Trevor had. "I'm terribly sorry, but Miss Melodie won't be able to speak to you. This is her governess." And then she hung up fast.

"Reporters," she said. "Three called yesterday. I don't know how they got our new number, but they did."

"Why would a reporter want to talk to you?" I asked.

"Don't be a fool," Melodie said, and suddenly she sounded old and bitter. "The word is out about the custody fight. So now, thanks to my wonderful parents, Lissa and I are celebrities."

And even I knew then that being a celebrity wasn't always pleasant.

Chapter

8

It seemed like a perfectly ordinary Friday night.

Miss Hardwick dropped Melodie and Lissa off at the usual time, and Mom asked Miss Hardwick if she'd like to stay for supper. Miss Hardwick said no, they exchanged pleasantries, and then Miss Hardwick left. Melodie and I talked for a little while with Barry and Mitch, and Lissa ran to the kitchen to help Mom and Dad. I had a few quick regrets about not having asked Steve to join us, but we had a date for Saturday night, and Mom and Dad preferred it if I didn't see him twice in a weekend. Pizza and a movie sounded better than a family dinner to both of us, so that was what we decided on.

Of course, if you looked at us carefully you could see this really wasn't that ordinary a Friday night. For one thing, Melodie looked terrible. I'd never seen her look so bad. There were circles under her eyes, and she'd bitten off her fingernails. She'd also developed a habit of chewing on her lower lip.

And Mitch and Barry were much friendlier than usual before supper. You could see they were trying not to be too solicitous, as if someone in Melodie's family had died, but they made every effort to include us in their conversation. They even tried to talk about things that were interesting to Melodie, topics other than baseball and chess and trumpet-playing. Melodie tried, too, but her heart wasn't in it. Mine wasn't, either. Still, I really appreciated the twins' effort. I refused to believe I'd misjudged them all those years, so I decided they were improving with age. It was a nice idea.

After a while the strain of making conversation got to be too much for Melodie and me, so we went to the kitchen to volunteer our services. The twins and I help out almost every day, so Friday nights Mom and Dad give us the evening off. But they like it if we offer to help.

Mom put us to work immediately on the salad. I peeled and Melodie sliced. Dad was setting the table, and Mom was busy stirring and puttering. Lissa sat at the kitchen table, watching us all.

"Oh, I've been meaning to tell you something," I said to Melodie.

"Yeah, what?" she asked.

"I saw this really cute toy," I said. I'd decided the best way of finding out if Mom was interested—and still surprising her—was to involve her only indirectly in the conversation. "It was a model of a UFO."

I hadn't let Melodie in on my plans, so she looked at me strangely. "That sounds interesting," she said finally.

"It was," I said. "It had all kinds of UFO attachments and windows, and lots of other stuff." I tried to remember just what, but I'd paid more attention to the price tag than anything else.

"I've never seen a UFO model," Melodie said. "Have you, Doris?"

'No, I don't think so," Mom said. "It sounds interesting."

I decided not to push it any further. If Mom said it sounded interesting, that was good enough for me. I gave Melodie a wink to thank her, and she winked back.

"Tell me more about UFOs," Lissa said. "Doris, tell me about UFOs again, please."

"UFOs are ships that come from planets far away," Mom said, with that dreamy look she gets when some sucker asks her the right question. "They come to earth to look us over, and maybe get to know us."

"You've never seen a UFO, have you, Doris?" Lissa asked.

"No one has," I muttered.

"That's not true, Elaine," Mom said. "I may never have seen one, but lots of people have. If only the government would open its files, we'd see that a lot of very reliable people have reported seeing UFOs. Maybe some of the people with license plates like mine."

"Mom's license plate has UFO on it," I said to a puzzled-looking Lissa.

"Oh," Lissa said. "What happens to the UFOs when they leave earth? Where do they go then?"

"They must go home," Mom said. "Back to their own planets."

"Do they ever take Earth people with them?" Lissa asked.

"Some people have disappeared under very mysterious circumstances," Mom said. "And maybe they

81

did go away on the UFOs. Of course, unless they get back in touch with us, there's no way we can ever know."

"That's such garbage," I said. "Only crazy people believe junk like that."

"Don't talk to your mother that way," Dad said, walking into the kitchen. "Maybe UFOs exist, and maybe they don't, but it's an open question. You certainly don't have to be crazy to believe in them."

"Do you believe in UFOs?" Lissa asked him.

"I do," Dad said. "Doris has convinced me there is something to them. I hope someday I get to see one."

"There, now," Mom said. "You don't think your father and I are both crazy, do you, Elaine?"

I certainly did, but I also knew I'd be the crazy one if I admitted it. So I just shrugged my shoulders and let Melodie tactfully change the subject to Dad's plans for his garden.

Things went pretty smoothly at dinner. Mitch and Barry carried more than their share of conversation, but that's the way it usually is. Lissa seemed a little quiet to me, but I knew how upset she was about her parents, and that probably was the reason. Melodie listened a lot, too, but she talked when the conversation drifted her way. And if I was more quiet than usual, I'm sure Mom and Dad appreciated it.

We had just cleared off the dessert dishes when the doorbell rang. "Oh, no," Melodie murmured.

"Do you think it's Daddy?" Lissa asked, her eyes lighting up.

"I'll get it," Dad said.

"It might be a reporter," Melodie said, as he got

up. "They've been all over lately. If it's a reporter, please don't let him in."

"Don't worry," Dad said. "It's probably nothing. A stray insurance salesman."

"Or a UFO," I said, trying to sound funny, but sounding flat instead.

You can't see the front door from the dining room, but sounds carry well in my house. So we could hear Dad open the door and say, "Hans!" in a surprised voice.

"Hans?" Melodie asked. "You don't think something's the matter with Mama, do you?"

"Don't panic, Melodie," Mom said, but it was too late. Melodie had already leaped out of her chair and was running to the front hallway. I followed her, and Mom followed me. Eventually we all ended up in the living room.

"What is it, Hans?" Mom asked.

"Dr. Zuckerman," Hans said formally, "I have come for the children."

"What are you talking about?" Mom asked. "What children?"

Hans gave Mom a withering look. "Melodie and Lissa," he said, very slowly. I'm surprised he didn't point them out to her. "Mrs. Ashford has asked me to pick up the children and take them home."

"No," Melodie said, sitting down on the sofa. "I'm not going."

"Me, either," Lissa said, plopping down next to Melodie.

"This is ridiculous," Mom said. "Hans, Connie hasn't said anything to me about sending the girls

83

home tonight. Miss Hardwick was over earlier and she didn't say anything. The girls have overnight things here, and I can see no reason to send them away."

"There's been a change of plans," Hans said. "Mrs. Ashford has decided to send the girls to Boston for a few days to stay with their grandparents. They are to leave first thing tomorrow morning, so they should spend tonight at home, where they can pack their clothes and schoolbooks."

"Do you know anything about this?" Mom asked Melodie.

Melodie looked frantic. "Mama planned for us to go to Boston this weekend a while ago," she said. "But then there was that big mix-up about last weekend, and she hasn't mentioned anything to me since. Honest."

"I believe you, honey," Mom said. "I'm sorry, Hans, but I simply can't send the girls back unless I've spoken to Connie first. As long as they're in my house, they're my responsibility. And, frankly, I'm getting tired of having them whisked away from me at the ring of a doorbell."

"Hear, hear," Barry whispered. I don't think anyone else heard him, but I smiled.

"Why don't we call Connie now?" Dad said. "And get this all straightened out. We certainly don't want to keep the girls against her will."

Melodie looked at her watch. "Mom's in the middle of Act One," she said.

"All right, then," Dad said. "We'll call and leave a message for Connie to call after the show is over. In the meantime, we'll wait."

"But that will be too late," Hans said. "The girls must pack so we can leave early tomorrow. It's a long drive to Boston."

"So you'll get there a little later," Mom said. "I'm going to call Connie. In the meantime, Hans, would you like something to eat or drink? We still have some cake on the table."

"No, thank you," he said. He looked like eating our food would give him food poisoning.

"Well, make yourself at home," Mom said, and walked to the kitchen. The rest of us looked at one another and then sat down. We could hear Mom talking in the background, leaving her message.

"There," Mom said, joining us. "That's done. Are you sure you wouldn't like something, Hans? Tea or coffee?"

"No, thank you," he said.

"This is a scheme of Mama's," Melodie said. "She's going to send us to Boston to live with Gran and Grandad. We'll go to school there, and we'll never get to see Daddy."

"You don't know that," Mom said. "It's probably just a weekend visit, the way Connie originally planned. I'm sure your grandparents are upset about all this, the way everybody is. They must want to see you a lot."

"It's a plan," Melodie said. "You don't know the way Mama's been lately. She doesn't want Daddy anywhere near us. She'll do anything to keep him from us."

"I want Daddy," Lissa said, and started crying.

"Melodie!" Mom said sharply. She went over to Lissa and started cradling her.

"Your parents both want what's best for you," Dad said to Melodie. "They just have different opinions about what that is."

"That isn't true," Melodie said. "All they want is to get even with each other. If they cared about Lissa and me, they wouldn't keep doing this to us. They say terrible things about each other to us. It doesn't matter whether they're lies or truths, they just say things. And now they're fighting in public, and the newspapers know and they keep sending reporters over to ask us questions. It isn't so bad if they bother me, but they're going after Lissa, too. Some TV reporter stuck a microphone under Lissa's nose yesterday and asked her about Mom and Dad. Right at the playground."

"Then maybe going to Boston is a good idea," Dad said. "Maybe you girls should go away until the newspapers get interested in something else."

"That's fine for now," Melodie said. "But what about when the case goes to court? What then? What if the judge makes us testify, makes us pick between Mama and Daddy?"

"I don't want to pick!" Lissa cried.

"You won't have to," Mom said. "Judges don't put that kind of burden on kids. The judge will talk to you, but you won't have to decide."

"So somebody else gets to decide for me," Melodie said. "Is that any better?"

Mom sighed. "Probably not," she said. "I don't know, Melodie. All I do know is both your parents tend to get a little . . . carried away when they're upset. And you don't help matters any when you get carried away, too. You're only adding to Lissa's tensions with your own."

"I'm fifteen years old," Melodie said. "I'm not grown up, either. Why do I have to be the one to deal with Mama's craziness and Daddy's craziness and not add to Lissa's tensions at the same time? What about my tensions? I just wish they'd all drop dead!"

That only made Lissa cry harder. Mom tried to reach out to Melodie, but she'd already gotten up and run upstairs. I started to follow her but Mom told me not to. "Give her a chance to calm down," Mom said. "I can see this is going to be a long night."

I would have loved to blame it all on Hans, who was sitting comfortably on a straight-backed chair, trying to act unaware of all the screaming around him, but I knew that was unfair. Connie had had one of her sudden brilliant ideas and ordered him to come over. I could remember when Connie's brilliant ideas had been for picnics and unplanned trips to New York. I used to really like Connie.

"Can I turn on the TV?" Mitch asked.

"I think that's a wonderful idea," Mom said. "Something we can all watch."

Mitch picked a baseball game, but that was okay, too. Anything dramatic might have been too upsetting, and none of us was in the mood for a comedy.

After an hour Melodie came back downstairs. "I'm sorry," she said.

"I'm sorry, too," Mom said. "Sometimes I forget you aren't all grown up. You have every right to be upset."

"I want Melodie to sit next to me," Lissa said, so

Melodie joined her. We watched the game in relative silence, one of us occasionally getting up to get a piece of fruit or go to the bathroom. I made one trip to the kitchen and found myself relieved to be away from the tension of the living room. It took a real effort to make myself go back there.

The game ended and the phone rang at almost the same moment. Mom got up, turned off the set, and walked to the kitchen to answer the phone. Melodie followed her, getting up carefully so she wouldn't disturb Lissa, who had fallen asleep on the sofa. I walked to the kitchen just behind Melodie.

"Yes, Connie," Mom said. "Yes, I understand, but you've got to understand, too. . . . Well, I'm sorry if it interfered with your plans, but I just couldn't send the girls out without speaking to you first. . . . Yes, it's true, I did last week, but that was different. . . . Well, for one thing, that was their father, not their chauffeur. . . . Yes, Connie. . . . Yes, I understand that, Connie. . . . No, Connie, that simply isn't true. . . . Connie, I know you're upset about all this. Believe me, we're all upset. . . . Look, there isn't any damage here. Lissa is asleep, but if you want, I'll wake her and the girls can go back right now. . . . Yes, I understand. . . . Connie, I really wish you'd think about that. . . . Connie, I'm sure when you calm down, you'll change your mind about that. . . . Now stop it, Connie, I'm not talking like a dentist! . . . Connie! . . . Very well, if that's the way you feel about it, but you're making a big mistake, and the girls are the ones who'll be hurt." And then Mom hung up. She looked grim.

"Melodie, wake Lissa," Mom said. "Try not to show her you're upset. Your mother wants you girls to go home right now with Hans."

"I'm up," Lissa said, walking to the kitchen. She was rubbing her eyes and looked sweet and rumpled. "I don't want to go."

"I'm afraid you have to, honey," Mom said, and bent down to kiss Lissa's hair. "You'll be home in bed in just a few minutes."

"I don't want to," Lissa repeated.

"What were you so upset about?" Melodie asked Mom. "What did Mama say to you?"

"It can wait," Mom said. "Besides, I'm sure once Connie calms down, she'll change her mind."

"I want to know, Doris," Melodie said. "If it has anything to do with me, I have the right to know."

"I'm sick and tired of everybody's rights in this matter," Mom said. "Your mother said she would prefer it if you girls didn't spend so much time here. That's all."

"She didn't say that," Melodie told Mom. "You're covering up. She said she doesn't want us to come here ever again, didn't she?"

"Not quite in those words," Mom answered. "Besides, you know your mother."

"Oh, yeah," Melodie said. I never thought she could sound so harsh. "Oh, I know Mama all right. Anybody want to make a bet I never see you again?"

Chapter
9

Saturday mornings my parents go to synagogue. Mitch and Barry and I don't have to, but lots of times we go with them, and sometimes Melodie and Lissa come, too. I guess the twins and I felt the need for a little religion that Saturday, or maybe just a sense of family after the night before, because we were all dressed and eating breakfast when the phone rang. I was closest, so I answered it.

"Elaine, have you seen Lissa?"

It was Melodie and she sounded upset. "Of course not," I said. "Not since last night. Why?"

"She's missing," Melodie said. "She isn't in her room or anyplace else I can think of."

"Maybe she got up early and went for a walk," I suggested.

"Lissa's been so upset lately," Melodie said. "Elaine, I'm scared."

"You should talk to Mom," I said. "I'll get on the extension."

"All right," Melodie said, and I handed the phone to Mom. Melodie must have explained the situation to her while I was walking into the den, because Mom was trying to calm her down by the time I picked up the extension.

"Hans is furious," Melodie said. "Marta looked for Lissa with me, but Hans is sulking because the trip's been delayed. He's convinced Lissa is just playing a game, hiding in a closet or bathroom somewhere."

"It's possible she is," Mom said. "Not a game exactly, but we know she doesn't want to go to Boston. Have you checked the house thoroughly?"

"Marta and I have," Melodie said. "Miss Hardwick has the weekend off. She's supposed to meet us in Boston on Monday. We've looked every—oh, hold on a second, would you?"

So Mom and I held on. Maybe Marta had located Lissa, after all. The Ashfords had such a gift for dramatizing.

But when Melodie got on the phone, it was obvious Lissa hadn't been found. I recognized the tone in Melodie's voice. It was her I-don't-care, I-will-not-cry voice.

"Lissa's run away," she said. "She left a note on Mama's bed, of all places. Like Mama would care."

"Of course Connie would care," Mom said sharply. "What does the note say?"

" 'Dear Mama,' " Melodie read. " 'I don't like it here anymore. I am going away on a UFO. Love, Lissa.' "

"Oh, no," Mom said.

"Mom, I told you not to fill her head with those stupid fantasies," I said sharply.

"That's not important," Melodie said. "Doris, what should I do?"

"We'll start looking for her right away," Mom said. "You call your parents and let them know."

"What can they do?" Melodie asked. "Mama's in New York for the weekend, and she has a show at two o'clock. And Daddy's in L.A., and he isn't supposed to come home until this evening."

"You didn't say anything about that yesterday," I said.

"I didn't know yesterday," Melodie said. "I found out this morning when I called Daddy to see if he'd swiped Lissa last night when none of us was looking. He flew out yesterday morning without telling us."

"Your mother should be told," Doris said. "If you want I'll call her."

"I don't think that's a great idea," Melodie said. "I think I'll wait awhile and see if we can find Lissa. If we haven't found her by the time the matinee is through, then I'll call her. She won't come home, anyway."

"Do you want to call the police?" Mom asked.

"No," Melodie said. "Not unless we have to. Not until Mama says we should. I can't bear the idea of more publicity."

"All right," Mom said. "We'll go looking for her around here, and Hans and Marta can look in your neighborhood. You stay by your phone, and I'll stay by mine, in case Lissa calls or somebody finds her. And don't worry, honey. Kids run away all the time, and then show up sound asleep in bed."

"Okay," Melodie said. "Call me if you hear anything."

"Don't worry, we will," Mom said, and we all hung

up. Mom and I went back to the kitchen, and Mom told everybody what was going on.

"I'll take my car," Dad said, "since it's in the driveway, and cover the mall area. Lissa might have taken a bus over there. The mall isn't open yet, but she could be hanging around."

"Good idea," Mom said. "Call if you find her."

"Of course," Dad said, and after he checked to make sure he had his car keys, he left.

"I'll bike over to the elementary school," Mitch said, "and check the playground."

"I'll check the park," Barry said. "Lissa might be playing there."

"I'm going to call Steve," I said. "He can check out his neighborhood, while I look around here."

"You go on, I'll call Steve," Mom said. "I'll do it faster."

I was still mad at her for filling Lissa's mind with those dumb UFOs, so I just grunted okay and left the house. The twins had brought my bike out from the garage, so I got right on and started riding around the block.

I checked everywhere I could think of without any luck. Then I decided to scout the shops in the downtown area. I was as thorough as I could be, even checking the ladies' room in the different diners and fast food places. No Lissa.

What was frustrating was knowing that Lissa could have been anyplace ten minutes before, and I could have just missed her. Wherever I went I asked if people had seen her, trying to sound casual about it, and I showed them the picture of Lissa that I carried around in my wallet. Nobody remembered seeing her.

After a couple of hours, I called home, but Mom said there was no news. Everyone else was calling in, too, so we all knew we had to keep looking.

I started going over the same turf again, just in case Lissa had gone there since I'd last looked. And this time I looked even more carefully, checking places Lissa was unlikely to go to. Barber shops. grocery stores, laundromats. Anyplace with a door, I went into. Lissa wasn't in any of them, and nobody could remember seeing her. I started to think Lissa really had found a UFO.

I found another phone booth and called home again.

"Nothing," Mom said. "I think we should call the police, but Melodie refuses. And it's too late now to call Connie—her matinee has already started."

"Is it that late?" I asked, and then looked at my watch. It was two-ten. No wonder I was so hungry.

"I really wish Miss Hardwick were around," Mom said. "She probably knows Lissa better than any of us. And she could talk sense into Melodie, which I don't seem able to do."

"I'm going over to Melodie's," I said. "She must be going crazy all alone."

"Do that," Mom said. "Melodie could use you right now. And if the two of you swap ideas, you might come up with something."

"Okay," I said, and hung up. It was a long bike ride to Melodie's house from downtown, and while I biked I tried to think of where Lissa might be. Every blond girl I saw I thought was her, and one of them I even called out to, only to find it was somebody else. I was too tired and hungry and worried to be embarrassed.

Melodie opened the door and, without even thinking about it, I hugged her. She looked so sad and frightened.

"I don't know where she could be," Melodie said. "I've been searching the house over and over just in case she's hidden someplace sneaky, but I haven't found her. And nobody's called me, and your mother has been really sweet, but I can tell she thinks I'm wrong not to call the police or tell Mama."

"So why don't you tell your mother?" I asked. "This really is an emergency."

"Because if I get her on the phone, I'll scream at her," Melodie said. "This is her fault and Daddy's, and I just want to kill them for making Lissa so unhappy."

"Mom could call her," I said. "She really thinks Connie should know."

"I'm not sure Mama would even take a call from your mother," Melodie said. "Mama called here after we got home last night, and she was furious at your parents for keeping us at your house."

I wanted to say I thought Connie was crazy, but she was Melodie's mother. So I tried to think of something else to say, and I realized again how hungry I was.

"Is there anything for me to eat?" I asked. "I skipped lunch while I was looking."

"Oh, poor Elaine," Melodie said. "Of course there is." So we went to the kitchen and got out stuff for a sandwich.

Something about the refrigerator bothered me, and then I realized what it was.

I thought for a moment about keeping it to myself,

but I knew if I was right, Melodie would find out soon enough. "Do you still have that freezer in your basement?" I asked, trying to sound casual.

"Sure," Melodie said. "Why?"

"I know this is dumb," I said. "But maybe . . ."

"Lissa might have hidden in the freezer?" Melodie asked. "Oh, Elaine, you don't think so?"

"No, of course not," I said. "But we should check it out, just in case."

"Lissa doesn't even like the basement," Melodie said, as we started down the stairs. "I checked here earlier, but I didn't think about the freezer."

"But kids do dumb stuff like hide in freezers sometimes. You read about it in the papers."

"You read about it if they find the kids dead," Melodie said. Then we ran to the freezer. It looked like a giant white coffin. Connie had bought it when meat prices had started to rise, but it hadn't been used in years. I didn't know whether that was good or not.

"I can't open it," Melodie whispered. "I can't look."

So I opened it. I closed my eyes, praying Lissa would jump out, yelling, "Surprise!" But when there was no yell, I opened my eyes and looked. Lissa wasn't there.

"It's okay," I said, not sure whether to laugh or cry. "Lissa isn't in there."

"Thank God," Melodie said, but she peeked in just to be sure. "She could have died in there."

"I'm sorry I even mentioned it," I said. "I should have checked first, and then you wouldn't have had to worry at all."

"You didn't eat your sandwich," Melodie said, as we stood there staring at the freezer.

"Have you eaten?" I asked, closing the freezer door. "I bet you haven't eaten a thing all day."

"I haven't wanted to," Melodie said. "Come on. You eat your sandwich, and I'll have an apple."

"Deal," I said, and we started up the stairs. When we reached the hallway we heard the phone ringing. Melodie flew to it.

I ran after her, but by the time I reached her I could tell it wasn't good news. "Okay, I'll call her," Melodie was saying as I got there. She hung up and turned to face me.

"Nothing," she said. "The longer we take to find her, the worse it gets."

"We'll find her," I said.

Melodie ignored me. "Eat your sandwich," she said. "I have to call Mama. It should be intermission now. I'll do it from the study."

"Do you want me to join you in there?" I asked. "Maybe talk to your mother, too?"

"No, I'd better do this alone," Melodie said. "Eat your sandwich and rest for a few minutes. You must be exhausted."

So I watched while she left the room, and then I ate my sandwich. At first it was hard getting it down, but hunger won out and soon I was wolfing it. Still, I didn't taste a thing.

It seemed to take forever for Melodie to get off the phone. She'd closed the study door, and I couldn't hear what she was saying. I resisted the temptation to pick up the kitchen phone and listen in, mostly because I was afraid of what Connie was saying about my mother. I might think this was all Mom's fault, but that didn't mean Connie had a right to.

It took about ten minutes for Melodie to come back to the kitchen. "Well, that's done," she said. "Mama was hysterical, of course, but she decided there was no point coming back here and missing tonight's performance."

"It's her job," I said. "And there isn't anything she can do."

"She could look," Melodie said. "She could sit by the phone and direct traffic the way your mother's been doing all day. She could care enough to come to some sort of compromise with Daddy and not just threaten to hide us away someplace where he can't find us."

"How much of that did you tell her?" I asked.

"Not as much as I should have," Melodie said. "I left a message with Daddy's service to call here the minute he gets home. I didn't want to say Lissa was missing, in case we find her, but at some point, he ought to be told she ran away. If Mama knows, Daddy has to know. Equal rights."

"I'm going to start looking again," I said. "You don't need me here anymore."

"Okay," Melodie said. "I'm going to call your mother to tell her what Mama said."

"Did she say to call the police?" I asked, as I stood by the kitchen door.

"No, of course not," Melodie said. "She thinks if it makes the papers, Daddy will use it against her."

"I'll see you later," I promised. I felt bad leaving, but there was nothing I could do there. Besides, maybe I'd find something between Melodie's house and mine.

But the main reason I wanted to go home was that I wanted to have it out with Mom. I knew Trevor and Connie were mostly to blame, but it was about time Mom realized she was at fault, too.

I saw no sign of Lissa as I biked home. I left my bike by the front door and charged into the house.

Mom was on the phone when I got in, and I held my breath, praying that it was someone saying Lissa had been found. But Mom hung up and shook her head.

"I know you're not completely at fault," I said. "But Lissa never would have run away if you hadn't fed her those stupid stories."

"Elaine, I am in no mood for your accusations," Mom said.

"I don't care what kind of mood you're in," I said. "Lissa's scared and unhappy and she'll believe anything you tell her. You knew how unhappy she was. You knew how much she needed to escape. But you kept on telling her, anyway."

"Elaine, please," Mom said. "After we find Lissa, then we'll talk this out. You do have a point, and I do feel bad. But this isn't the time."

"Sure," I said. "When you want to talk about your precious UFOs it's just fine. But if I want to—"

"Enough, Elaine," Mom said sharply. "We're both upset, and screaming won't help us find Lissa."

"A lot you care," I said, but I knew that was a lie. "Dumb UFOs," I continued. "Dumb UFOs."

And then it came to me.

"Mom, where's your car?" I asked.

"In the garage," Mom said. "Why?"

"Has anyone checked it?" I asked, and I could hardly keep the excitement out of my voice.

"No," Mom said. "Oh, Elaine, you don't think—"

But before she even finished the question, we'd both started for the garage. Mom got there first and opened the garage door, but I beat her to the car. The green Datsun, license plate UFO 86, stood there silently.

And equally silent, curled up in a ball and sound asleep on the back seat, lay Lissa.

Chapter
10

I won't go to Boston" were Lissa's first words when we woke her up to get her out of the car. She whined, too, and then demanded something to eat. I suppose she figured she wasn't lost and there was no reason to be grateful to us for finding her. But I would have appreciated some kind of thanks.

Hans drove Melodie over as soon as Mom had called her. I think of all of us he was in the worst mood.

"No discipline," he muttered, as he stood in the living room. "The children are spoiled rotten by their parents. A little discipline, and we could have been in Boston already."

"Thank you, Hans," Dad said. "I'll be sure to mention that to the Ashfords."

"They know already," Hans said. "They just choose to ignore the truth."

"We'd invite you to stay, Hans," Mom said, "but right now we just can't deal with anyone except Melodie and Lissa. I'm sure you understand."

"All they need is a good spanking," Hans said, but at least he left without an argument.

I thought Melodie and Lissa would rush into each other's arms, and at least the two of them would be happy, but the moment Melodie spotted Lissa she started screaming at her.

"Are you crazy?" she cried. "Do you know how much you scared all of us? I searched in the freezer for you! I was convinced I'd find you dead. And you ruined everybody's day. The Zuckermans spent the day searching for you. So did Steve, and Hans and Marta. And Daddy and Mama had to be told, and they're both very upset with you and I hope they give you just what you deserve."

Lissa started to cry, and even I felt sorry for her. I had never heard Melodie raise her voice to her, and I had a feeling neither had Lissa.

"I didn't mean to be bad," Lissa whispered. "But I couldn't go to Boston."

"You acted like a spoiled brat," Melodie said and turned away from Lissa. I could see she was shaking with anger and relief. Lissa kept crying, and it was obvious Melodie wanted to comfort her but she was holding herself back. After a minute, I couldn't stand being in the same room with them, so I walked to the kitchen as inconspicuously as possible. Steve, who'd come over when the search ended, followed me.

"Fun date," he said. "A real Saturday night special."

"Oh, Steve," I said, but I started giggling.

"Are all your parties this much fun?" he asked, and then he started laughing, too. Soon we were in each other's arms, weak from laughter.

Dad walked in then, and I thought he might say

something about us hugging, but he just said, "It's been one crazy day, all right," and went over to the refrigerator. He took out some cheddar cheese, then got a knife and started slicing it. I was so hungry even cheddar cheese looked good, and Dad sliced some for Steve and me, too.

"I ought to get us something for supper," Dad said, as we finished the cheese. "Pick up a pizza."

"That sounds good," I said.

"Mom is very upset about something," Dad said, trying to sound casual. "Do you know what it is, Elaine?"

"I think she feels bad because she told Lissa those UFO stories," I said. "We talked about it earlier."

"I hope you didn't blame her," Dad said.

"Do we have to talk about this in front of Steve?" I asked.

"I guess not," Dad said. "But we do have to talk about it at some point."

"Not now," I said, and then I remembered how Mom had said the same thing to me and I'd kept at her anyway. "Look, maybe I was too rough on Mom. But I was angry and upset, and I do think she was wrong to fill Lissa's head with those dumb stories."

"Your mother loves those dumb stories," Dad said. "You think it's all that fascinating being a dentist? You think you and the twins provide her with enough excitement? You think she gets her kicks through my adventures with computer chips?"

"Couldn't she find something else to interest her?" I asked. "Sky diving, maybe, or mountain climbing."

"Your mother has a beautiful, lively imagination,"

Dad said. "It's one of the things I love best about her. And I hope when you grow up enough, you'll learn to appreciate it, too, and not put her down because she thinks there's more to this universe than suburbia."

"I wish my mother had an imagination like that," Steve said. "Her idea of creativity is to put nuts in the chocolate chip cookies."

I tried to smile, but Dad wasn't amused. "I don't know what parents have to do to impress their kids," he said. "We try so hard—yes, even Trevor and Connie—and all we get is criticism."

"I'm sorry, Dad," I said, although I wasn't quite sure why I was apologizing. Dad was always saying how crazy his own mother was, and all she did was play the stock market.

"We're all tired," Dad said. "It's been a long day, and I have a feeling it's going to be a long night, too. Steve, can you stay for pizza?"

"If it's okay with Elaine," he said, and I nodded. Dad went back to the living room and got orders for the pizza. I could hear Barry and Mitch rejecting anchovies.

"You don't really wish your mother was like mine, do you?" I asked Steve.

"Not completely," Steve said. "I don't like cheddar cheese that much. But Mom is so housebound. She likes being a housewife, and I guess it's okay, but things would be easier financially if she had a job. And I think maybe she'd be happier getting out more. But I guess she's scared to."

"I don't think Mom is scared of anything," I said. "Except tooth decay."

"Nobody's mother is perfect," Steve said. "No one's family is."

"Hmm," I said. "That's exactly what Melodie said to me. When are we all going to believe it?"

This time when we hugged, it wasn't from laughter. And Dad just ignored us as he walked through to the back door.

Steve left around nine, and Lissa went to bed right after that. The rest of us sat in the living room, not talking very much, pretending to watch TV and waiting for Trevor to call.

Only he didn't call; he came over straight from the airport. He'd checked in with his service as soon as he'd landed and gotten a half-dozen messages about Lissa. By the time he got the last one, he was completely confused and decided the best thing was to come straight to our house and check on Lissa for himself.

"She looks fine to me," he said, as he joined us in the living room. "Sleeping like an angel."

"Some angel," Melodie said.

"It isn't my place to say anything," Mom said.

"Nonsense, Doris," Trevor said. "We've thrown our problems straight into your lap. You have every right to speak."

"I just want to say . . ." Mom began, but then she was silent. "No, it can wait. What I have to say, I have to say to you and Connie together."

"Ah, yes," Trevor said. "Connie. I don't suppose you know what her plans are for this evening?"

"She's coming over later," Melodie said. "Hans drove into the city to bring her here."

I hoped he'd stay in the car. I didn't think I could take his little lessons on discipline twice in one night.

"I can't believe she left you all alone to handle this crisis," Trevor said to Melodie. "You're scarcely more than a child yourself."

"You weren't here, either," Melodie said.

"That's different," he said. "I didn't know anything had happened until after the plane landed. It was hardly my fault I was three thousand miles away."

"Of course it was your fault," Melodie said. "All this is your fault and Mama's. Neither of you is ever around when we need you. And when you do show up, it's to cause problems. To scream at each other. To whisk us away to New York or Boston or wherever it suits you."

"Really, Melodie," Trevor said. "I'm sure the Zuckermans have no desire to hear any of this."

"They've heard worse," Melodie said. "I swear, sometimes I feel closer to them than I do to you and Mama. They're here for us the way you aren't. They were the ones to search for Lissa. They were the ones to find her. Lissa sleeps better when she's here, did you know that? She has horrible nightmares at home, but here she sleeps through the night. How does that make you feel?"

"That shows me it's all the more important for me to carry on the custody suit," Trevor said. "Clearly the problem is Connie and her inability as a mother. I'm horrified that I ever trusted her with the guardianship of my daughters. I just hope I'm not too late to undo the damage she's done."

"I give up," Melodie said. She sat back in her chair, folded her arms, and withdrew.

"I hope when this case reaches the courts I can count on your help," Trevor said to Mom and Dad. "I'm sure your testimony will be a great help to me in my fight to save my children."

"Don and I both hope it won't reach the courts," Mom said. "It's not too late for you and Connie to settle this peacefully."

"You've got to give it a try," Dad said. "For the sake of the kids."

"Don't tell me that," Trevor said. "Connie's the one who's being irrational."

"If you'll excuse us," Barry said, "Mitch and I are both tired, and we've had enough family squabbling for one day. Good night, everybody."

It usually drives me crazy when one of the twins speaks for both of them, but this time it didn't bother me. We said good night and watched as they walked up the stairs.

"Elaine," Mom said, "do you want to go to bed now, too?"

"No," Melodie said. "I want her here with me when Mama comes."

"Melodie, it might be better if you went to bed, also," Mom said. "Your mother is going to be tired and upset when she gets here, and I don't see how your presence is going to make things easier."

"I'm not going to bed until after I've seen her," Melodie said. "And it's important for me to have Elaine here. Elaine's been through all of this with me. She knows everything that's gone on, and I need her here."

"I'm not tired," I lied. The truth was, I was exhausted, but I was also aware I'd never fall asleep with all that tension in and around me. And if Melodie thought I could help her, I was certainly willing to try.

We didn't have long to wait. Connie made her entrance a few minutes later. Hans must have broken all the speed limits to get her here that fast.

"Where's my baby?" she cried, only she didn't wait for Mom's answer. She just ran upstairs and found her way to the guest room. Trevor scowled and Melodie looked disgusted, but I felt relieved. At least Connie still had her sense of the dramatic.

"She looks so peaceful," Connie said when she finally joined us. "That precious child. How she must have suffered."

"That's just what we were discussing," Trevor said. "How the children are suffering under your care."

"My care?" Connie said. "Lissa never knows from one minute to the next when you're going to steal her, and you say all this is my fault?"

"Stop it!" Mom shouted.

She was so loud we all turned around and looked at her in shock.

"Just stop it," she said, more quietly this time. "Trevor, Connie, I love you both, and I'm sure you're enjoying the theatrics of the moment, but I have some simple truths I want to say to both of you."

"Ah," Trevor said. "The scolding."

"Only children get scolded," Mom said. "If this feels like a scolding, it's probably because you're behaving like children."

"Really, Doris," Connie said. "I know you're a bit

irritated with me, and I do apologize, but you must understand how upset I was. And you have to admit that if you'd let Hans take the girls last night, none of this would have happened."

"I admit I was partly at fault," Mom said. "Although I'd do the same thing again if the situation arose. I take my responsibility to Melodie and Lissa very seriously, and when they're under my roof they're under my protection. I should think you'd appreciate that."

"We do," Trevor said. "If Connie weren't so thoughtless—"

"I'm thoughtless!" Connie shouted. "As though I were the one who flew off to California and didn't even bother telling anyone in case an emergency arose!"

"Stop it, both of you," Dad said. "No wonder Lissa has nightmares. No wonder Melodie is scared to be in the same room with the two of you. You seem determined to make as big a mess of this as you possibly can."

"We were very lucky today," Mom said. "We found Lissa and she was all right. But can you imagine how many awful things could have happened? Lissa could have picked some other car to hide in. Or she could have figured out a way to hide in the trunk. Or I could have driven off without knowing she was in the car and parked someplace, and she could have gotten out and I never would have known. Or I could have started the car running in the garage, and who knows, the phone could have rung. I could have run to get it, leaving the motor on, and Lissa could have died of carbon monoxide poisoning. Any one of those things could have happened today, and we should just thank God none of them did."

"I'll have a serious talk with Lissa tomorrow," Connie said. "Thank you, Doris, for pointing all that out to us."

"I'm not through yet," Mom said. "Sure you should talk to Lissa. But first you should talk to Trevor."

"I have nothing to say to him," Connie said.

"You have a great deal to say to him," Mom said. "You have two daughters who are miserable over the way you've been behaving. Scolding Lissa isn't going to make a bit of difference unless you and Trevor start behaving differently. You're tearing your girls apart with your anger, and I know you don't want to do that. I know you love your daughters, and they love you still. But both of you are on the verge of losing their love and their respect, and, believe me, once that's lost, it's a lot harder to find than a runaway child."

Somewhere in the middle of all that I felt like crying. To think I'd been screaming at Mom about her UFOs when I'd never had a moment's doubt that I loved her and she loved me. I wondered if I could ever make it up to her, and then I realized that of course I could, and it wouldn't even be hard. A sincere apology and the words "I love you" would clear up the matter completely.

"I want to say something," Melodie said. "Daddy, Mama, I want you to really listen to me. Elaine and I have talked about this a lot, and we have at least part of a solution."

"We're listening," Trevor said.

"It seems to us that a lot of the problem is that Lissa and I are out here in Morganville while the two of you are working in New York," Melodie said. "That was okay when you were married, because one or another of you was almost always home, but now it's just Mama and she has to be in New York half the week for her work. And naturally you worry about us, Daddy, because you can't keep an eye on us out here and you know Mama isn't here, and something like what happened today could happen anytime."

"I would have come home immediately if there had been anything I could do," Connie said. "But there didn't seem to be, and if I did come back it would mean missing my evening show, and I couldn't do that because of a child's brattiness."

"Running away is hardly bratty," Trevor said.

"Stop it," Melodie said. "Stop using Lissa and me as an excuse to snipe at each other. How do you think that makes us feel?"

"You had an idea," Mom said gently. "I'd like to hear it."

"I know this isn't the solution to everything," Melodie said. "But I think it would help if Mama sold the house and we moved into New York."

"But I thought you loved it here," Connie said.

"I do," Melodie said. "But not like this. Not with all this anger. And it's hard for us to see either of you. If we were in the city we'd see more of you during the week, and it would be easier for us to see Daddy, too. If Mama is touring in a show, we can stay with Daddy and there won't be any problem with school. We can just take the subway."

"No daughter of mine will ever take the subway,"

111

Trevor said. But then he laughed. "What do you say, Connie? I think our daughter is a bloody genius, coming up with such a practical solution to all our problems."

"It hardly solves everything," Connie said. "But it would mean we'd have more of a chance to be with our daughters, and I know how important that is to me. And to you, too," she added quickly. "And I certainly wouldn't miss the commute. What do you think, Doris?"

"I think you should think about it," Mom said. "And the two of you should discuss it thoroughly. But not here and now. It's been an awfully long day, and nothing has to be decided this minute except where we're all going to sleep."

"I'm staying here," Melodie said.

"Fine," Connie said. "Trevor, why don't you use the guest room at my house? That way we can talk about all this privately tomorrow morning."

"Thank you," Trevor said. "That sounds like an excellent idea to me."

"May I go to bed now?" I asked, of nobody in particular. Melodie heard me, though, and she smiled and nodded.

I smiled, too, until I fell asleep.

Chapter

11

I can't believe I'm happy that you're moving away," I said to Melodie Wednesday afternoon. We were sitting on a park bench, soaking up the sun after school.

"It's not until the end of the school year," Melodie said. "And we wouldn't be seeing much of each other after that, anyway, now that Mama's agreed we can go to London this summer."

"That sounds like so much fun," I said.

"Work on your parents," Melodie said. "It sounded like they might be willing to let you come for a visit in July."

"I think there's a real chance of that," I said. "My parents like Penelope. And Mom and I are getting along great right now. I don't tease her about UFOs, and she's stopped putting cheddar cheese in everything."

"Besides, even when I live in New York, we'll see a lot of each other," Melodie said. "I'll come for visits, and you'll go to the city. And there's the phone, and letters."

"I know," I said. "But I will miss you."

"I'll miss you, too," Melodie said. "But it's for the best."

"Oh, I know," I said. "I just can't get over how quickly your parents worked out the details."

"Things still aren't perfect," Melodie said. "But they had a marathon session on Sunday, and I think they understand what they were doing and why. They'll still scream at each other occasionally, but they've always done that. At least now they talk sometimes, as well as scream."

"You're going to be sophisticated," I said, "living in New York. You'll never want to come here again."

"Honestly, Elaine," Melodie said. "What do you want, reassurance?"

"It wouldn't hurt," I said.

"I love you, and I love your family," Melodie said. "And I've had too many Friday night dinners at your house not to want some more."

"I believe you," I said. "It's just that I'll miss you like crazy."

"It *is* for the best, though," Melodie said. "Not just because it'll make things easier with Mama and Daddy. It'll be better for me because of your family."

"What do you mean?" I asked. "You just said you loved us all."

"I do," Melodie said. "That's the problem. I can't tell you how many times in the past couple of years I've wished I were a member of your family. I used to dream about living with you, having your parents adopt me somehow. Sometimes I threw in Lissa, but mostly it was just me."

"I can't imagine that," I said. "Your parents are so glamorous."

"They are," Melodie said. "And they do love me, and I love them. But your mother is so funny and alive, only without Mama's theatrics. And your father is always there for you."

"He's in Pittsburgh half the time," I said.

"But never when it counts," she said. "I'll never forget how he canceled his business trip to be with you when you had your tonsils out. Daddy was in Paris when mine were taken out. And even when your dad's in Pittsburgh, you can reach him. He can come back if he has to. I've always envied you that."

I thought about it. Dad had dropped everything when the twins' appendixes had to be taken out. I figured that was just because it was the twins, and sort of an emergency, but I couldn't remember a time when *I* needed Dad to be around and he wasn't.

And even the twins were okay. They helped search for Lissa. They'd talked with me when I needed advice about Melodie. For the first time, I realized I'd miss them when they left for college.

"Everybody's going away," I said finally. "Who will I have left?"

"You'll still have me," Steve said. I hadn't even noticed him walking toward us. He sat down next to me on the bench and took my hand.

"Don't leave," I said. "Not for a few years, okay?"

"We just got here," Steve said. "We're not planning on moving for a while."

I squeezed his hand for comfort. He held mine tighter after that.

"Have I thanked you, Steve, for searching for Lissa?" Melodie asked. "I know you were at it all day, and I appreciate it so much."

"You thanked me Saturday and Sunday and Monday and Tuesday," Steve said. "This is the first you've thanked me today."

"Remind me to thank you again tomorrow," Melodie said. "I'm glad I've gotten to know you better."

"I'm glad, too," Steve said. "Elaine kept saying you were worth knowing, and she was right."

"I'm right about lots of stuff," I said, feeling surrounded by love and enjoying the feeling. "It's just that nobody ever listens to me."

Steve and Melodie ignored me. "Hey, have you two decided what you're doing your bio project on?" Steve asked. "It's due in a couple of weeks."

"I'm doing mine on life on Mars," Melodie said.

"You're kidding," I said. "Not UFOs?"

"No, not UFOs," Melodie said. "Microorganisms. There's a lot of interesting material on whether any exist on Mars."

"That's funny," Steve said. "Because I'm doing mine on UFOs."

"This is ridiculous," I said. "I can't believe my mother's spawned a whole generation of you."

"Not really UFOs," Steve said, "but the efforts we've been making to contact life on other planets. Radio signals and stuff like that."

"What does that have to do with biology?" I asked.

"Life is life," Steve said. "And biology studies life."

"It sounds really interesting," Melodie said. "Are you going to show your report to Doris?"

"Are you kidding?" Steve said. "She's my technical advisor."

"So what are you doing your report on?" Melodie asked me. "Steve and I seem to have outer space pretty much covered."

"I'm doing mine on computers and nutrition," I said. "I'm calling it Computer Chips and Chocolate Chips."

"That's terrible," Melodie said.

"It beats cutting up frogs," I said. "Besides, Dad offered to help me with it. Mom said she was too busy, and now I know why."

"Speaking of chocolate chips," Steve said, "Mom baked a chocolate cake yesterday, if anybody wants to come over and have some."

"I can't," Melodie said. "My schoolwork has really fallen off the past few weeks. I'm spending this whole week trying to catch up."

"I'd better not, either," I said. "Mom's checking my teeth tomorrow. If she finds even a wisp of chocolate, it's back to cheddar cheese."

"That just means more for me," Steve said. "I suppose I'll survive."

"Now that I've reminded myself of schoolwork, I'm feeling guilty about it," Melodie said. "I think I'll start heading home."

"I'd better, too," Steve said. "Before that cake gets stale."

"So I'm being dumped," I said. "I don't care. I'll just go back to my perfect family and try to figure out if there really is a connection between computers and nutrition."

"You can always make one up," Steve said.

"I may have to," I said. We all got up.

"See you tomorrow," Melodie said, and started walking away. Steve and I waved good-bye to her, exchanged good-bye kisses, and then started off in our separate directions. Much as I loved both of them, being alone felt good. I counted tulips on my way home, and smelled the lilacs, and marveled that anything as splendid as spring could exist with so little help from people.

The twins were sprawled out in the living room when I got in. I stared at them for a moment, and realized I really was going to miss them when they were gone. When the moment was right, I decided, I'd tell them that.

"What are you doing?" I asked.

"Trig," Barry said.

"Physics," Mitch said.

"Need any help?" I asked. "I could distract you if you want."

"As a matter of fact, we've been wanting to talk to you," Barry said.

I couldn't remember a time the twins had actually *wanted* to talk to me. I sat down nervously, not knowing what to expect.

"Things have been so crazy around here that we never had a chance to tell you how proud we are of you," Barry said.

"Proud?" I squeaked.

"Proud," Mitch said. "Starting with Melodie, the way you've helped her sort things out."

"And supporting the idea that Connie sell the house," Barry said. "Even though we know you'd be happier if Melodie stayed here."

"And the way you figured out where Lissa was," Mitch said. "Making the connection between Mom's license plate and Lissa's note."

"Someone would have figured it out," I said.

"But you're the one who did," Mitch said. "And that's why we're proud of you."

"Nice going, Elaine Marissa," Barry said.

I would have said something, but my jaws seemed to have locked in an "O" of surprise. When they finally relaxed, I was grinning too hard to say thanks.

Dad had spent Tuesday night in Pittsburgh, but he was home for supper, which the twins and I made. Haddock, broccoli, and baked potatoes. The kind of meal a computer would be proud of. It also tasted pretty good, and we were enjoying the food and the company.

"How was your meeting last night?" I even asked Mom.

"It was very interesting," she said. "I told the story about Lissa and my license plate, and everybody agreed you were very smart to figure it out."

"Lucky guess," I said, but I was smiling.

"We discussed at what age we should tell people about UFOs," Mom said. "Whether it really was too much for a child to understand."

"What did you decide?" Dad asked, helping himself to more broccoli.

"That a little caution isn't such a bad idea," Mom said. "That you shouldn't feed escape stories to kids who need to escape. But, as for kids who have a healthy curiosity about the universe, it might make them even more interested and eager to learn."

"You seem to have had that effect on Melodie and Steve," I said.

"But not on you?" Mom asked, only she had a half-smile on her face.

"I'll put it to you this way," I said. "If something with seven legs and five eyes and a couple of heads should happen to stop me on the street and ask for directions, I'll be able to handle it better than most people, thanks to you."

We all laughed. I couldn't remember the last time I laughed about Mom and her UFOs and it wasn't a mean laugh.

"You laugh," Mom said, as though she hadn't been laughing, too. "But there was a very informative speaker at the meeting. He saw a UFO just last summer, and he brought along some pictures."

"Out of focus?" Barry asked.

"Less than usual," Mom said. "It looked a lot like a Frisbee."

"Maybe it was a Frisbee," Mitch said.

"Have you ever seen a Frisbee with windows?" Mom asked. "Clean windows at that. A lot cleaner than the windows are here."

"I think she's hinting," Barry said. "Okay, Mom, we'll wash them this week."

"Children are such a joy," Mom said. "Aren't they, Don?"

"They're certainly something," Dad said.

We were still laughing when the doorbell rang. "Who could that be?" Mom asked.

"Probably somebody coming to pick up Melodie and Lissa," Barry said. "Lately that's the only reason the doorbell rings."

"I'll get it," I said. Maybe it was Steve bringing over some cake. When I'm in a good mood, I have the most wonderful daydreams.

Only it wasn't Steve. It was a deliveryman. "Package for Dr. Zuckerman," he said.

"I'll get her," I said, but by that point everybody had left the living room and crowded into the hallway.

"Dr. Zuckerman?" the deliveryman asked Dad.

"She's the doctor," Dad said, pointing to Mom.

The deliveryman gave him a funny look, but he gave Mom the sheet to sign. She did, and he handed over a large, well-wrapped box.

"I don't know what it can be," Mom said, carrying it to the kitchen. "I didn't order anything. And it weighs a ton."

"Is there a card?" I asked.

"There seems to be," Mom said. "Scotch-taped to the box." She ripped off the wrapping paper and tore the envelope off the box.

"It's from Trevor and Connie," she said. "Listen. 'Thanks for your love, your support, and your understanding heart. We hope this helps you with your searches.' I wonder what that means."

"Open the box and find out," Dad said. "Before we all go crazy."

So Mom cut the box open. Inside rested a shiny new telescope.

"Don, look at this," Mom gasped. "Kids, isn't it gorgeous?"

"It's amazing," Barry said.

"There's an instruction booklet," Mitch said.

"That was so nice of them," Mom said. "What a beautiful present."

"You deserve it," Dad said. "And it's good to know Trevor and Connie both realize it."

"And are doing things together again," Mom said. "Oh, I can't wait to use it."

"There's a new moon tonight," I said. "And not a cloud in the sky. Couldn't we set it up right now?"

"It doesn't look hard to assemble," Barry said.

"A great night for sighting Frisbees," Mitch said. "Frisbees with clean windows, that is."

"What are we waiting for?" I asked. "Come on, Mom. You could be the first dentist to ever clean an alien's teeth."

"Do you think they know about cheddar cheese on Mars?" Barry asked.

"If they don't, Mom will tell them," Mitch said.

"The joys of children," Dad said. "Remember?"

"Only too well," Mom said. "Come on, guys. Let's get it assembled, and we can search the stars together."

And the funny thing was, it sounded wonderful.

About the Author

Susan Beth Pfeffer is the popular author of over a dozen books for young adults, among them the Apple paperback, *Truth or Dare*. She lives and works in Middletown, New York.